DEMAIN PUBL

Short Sharp Shocks!

Book 0: Dirty Paws - Dean M. Drinkel
Book 1: Patient K - Barbie Wilde
Book 2: The Stranger & The Ribbon – Tim Dry
Book 3: Asylum Of Shadows – Stephanie Ellis
Book 4: Monster Beach – Ritchie Valentine Smith
Book 5: Beasties & Other Stories – Martin Richmond
Book 6: Every Moon Atrocious – Emile-Louis Tomas Jouvet
Book 7: A Monster Met – Liz Tuckwell
Book 8: The Intruders & Other Stories – Jason D. Brawn
Book 9: The Other – David Youngquist
Book 10: Symphony Of Blood – Leah Crowley
Book 11: Shattered – Anthony Watson
Book 12: The Devil's Portion – Benedict J. Jones
Book 13: Cinders Of A Blind Man Who Could See – Kev Harrison
Book 14: Dulce Et Decorum Est – Dan Howarth
Book 15: Blood, Bears & Dolls – Allison Weir
Book 16: The Forest Is Hungry – Chris Stanley
Book 17: The Town That Feared Dusk – Calvin Demmer
Book 18: Night Of The Rider – Alyson Faye
Book 19: Isidora's Pawn – Erik Hofstatter
Book 20: Plain – D.T. Griffith
Book 21: Supermassive Black Mass – Matthew Davis
Book 22: Whispers Of The Sea (& Other Stories) – L. R. Bonehill
Book 23: Magic – Eric Nash
Book 24: The Plague – R.J. Meldrum
Book 25: Candy Corn – Kevin M. Folliard
Book 26: The Elixir – Lee Allen Howard

Book 27: Breaking The Habit – Yolanda Sfetsos
Book 28: Forfeit Tissue – C. C. Adams
Book 29: Crown Of Thorns – Trevor Kennedy
Book 30: The Encampment / Blood Memory – Zachary Ashford
Book 31: Dreams Of Lake Drukka / Exhumation – Mike Thorn
Book 32: Apples / Snail Trails – Russell Smeaton
Book 33: An Invitation To Darkness – Hailey Piper
Book 34: The Necessary Evils & Sick Girl – Dan Weatherer
Book 35: The Couvade – Joanna Koch
Book 36: The Camp Creeper & Other Stories – Dave Jeffery
Book 37: Flaying Sins – Ian Woodhead
Book 38: Hearts & Bones – Theresa Derwin
Book 39: The Unbeliever & The Intruder – Morgan K. Tanner
Book 40: The Coffin Walk – Richard Farren Barber
Book 41: The Straitjacket In The Woods – Kitty R. Kane
Book 42: Heart Of Stone – M. Brandon Robbins
Book 43: Bits – R.A. Busby
Book 44: Last Meal In Osaka & Other Stories – Gary Buller
Book 45: The One That Knows No Fear – Steve Stred
Book 46: The Birthday Girl & Other Stories – Christopher Beck
Book 47: Crowded House & Other Stories - S.J. Budd
Book 48: Hand To Mouth – Deborah Sheldon
Book 49: Moonlight Gunshot Mallet Flame / A Little Death – Alicia Hilton
Book 50: Dark Corners - David Charlesworth

Murder! Mystery! Mayhem!
Maggie Of My Heart – Alyson Faye
The Funeral Birds – Paula R.C. Readman
Cursed – Paul M. Feeney
The Bone Factory – Yolanda Sfetsos

Beats! Ballads! Blank Verse!
Book 1: Echoes From An Expired Earth – Allen Ashley
Book 2: Grave Goods – Cardinal Cox
Book 3: From Long Ago – Paul Woodward
Book 4: Laws Of Discord – William Clunie

Horror Novels & Novellas
House Of Wrax – Raven Dane
A Quiet Apocalypse – Dave Jeffery
And Blood Did Fall – Chad A. Clark
The Underclass – Dan Weatherer
Greenbeard – John Travis

General Fiction
Joe – Terry Grimwood
Finding Jericho – Dave Jeffery

Science Fiction Collections
Vistas – Chris Kelso

Horror Fiction Collections
Distant Frequencies – Frank Duffy
Where We Live – Tim Cooke
Night Voices – Paul Edwards & Frank Duffy

Anthologies

The Darkest Battlefield – Tales Of WW1/Horror

WHERE WE LIVE
BY TIM COOKE

© Demain 2020

COPYRIGHT INFORMATION

Entire contents copyright © 2020 Tim Cooke / Demain Publishing

Cover © 2020 Adrian Baldwin (www.adrianbaldwin.info)

First Published 2020

All rights reserved. No part of this publication may be reproduced, stored or transmitted in any form or by any means, electronic, mechanical, photocopying, recording, scanning or otherwise without written permission from the publisher. It is illegal to copy this book, post it to a website or distribute it by any other means without permission.

What follows is entirely a work of fiction. The names, characters and incidents portrayed in it are the work of the author's imagination. Any resemblance to actual persons, living or dead, events or localities is entirely co-incidental.

Tim Cooke asserts the moral right to be identified as the author of this work in its totality.

Designations used by companies to distinguish their products are often claimed as trademarks. All brand names and product names used in this book and on its cover are trade names, service marks, trademarks and registered trademarks of their respective owners. The publishers and the book are not associated with any product or vendor mentioned in this book. None of the companies within the book have endorsed the book.

For further information, please visit:

WEB: www.demainpublishing.com
TWITTER: @DemainPubUk
FACEBOOK: Demain Publishing
INSTAGRAM: demainpublishing

CONTENTS

KESTRELS & CROWS	9
THE DRIVE HOME	11
THE BOX OF KNOWLEDGE	19
AN ORKNEY SAGA	51
NIGHTS AT THE FACTORY	57
THE BENCH BENEATH THE TREES	79
THE DUNES	87
ASYLUM	105
ACKNOWLEDGEMENTS	119
BIOGRAPHY	121
ADRIAN BALDWIN (COVER ARTIST)	123
DEMAIN PUBLISHING	125

KESTRELS & CROWS

I was born to this town and raised on its edge. I loved its light and stone, its currents and routines painted in abrupt, colloquial language. There was tranquillity to this place then, not unlike that found on the motorway that skirts its northern border: an industrial artery. Everyone drove forward at similar speeds, slowing occasionally into queues of traffic, glancing left and right, catching glimpses of kestrels hovering over the verges. Then all of a sudden, we began to veer off in different directions, the sun beating down, illuminating previously hidden junctions and laybys—dead ends and fresh starts. Some of us continued to plough through hedges into farmers' fields, tearing lesions into blankets of corn, tumbling on into wilderness. We inspected the bones of dead crows and other birds, and considered the lay of the land. We felt the plates grinding, churning the town out of shape.

THE DRIVE HOME

I sit here now, aged thirty and a father of two, thinking back over time to the person I was then. My hopes and fears, dreams and nightmares, the people I loved. I remember, with good reason, a journey home from visiting my sister in London when I was about twelve. She was living with her husband in Golders Green, and my brother and I had spent the day playing FIFA in a kitchen I now recall, perhaps incorrectly, to have been tired and covered in dirt. We left the capital via the M4 and while driving between Swindon and Bristol darkness descended. It came in an instant, like a flash, as if a bulb had burst.

I always felt extraordinary warmth and comfort in the busy, familial space of the car; there was a calmness to the intermittent clusters of passing lights, vehicles, lamps, occasional sirens. But I had long feared, since an indescribably terrifying nightmare years before, something lurking behind the guardrail and hedgerows, deep in the gloom. A presence without shape or matter but equipped with incredible speed and agility. On this winter evening, it seemed to be tracking us, racing alongside the car and reaching, like a spectre, for the door handle.

The bridge over to Wales was lit up like a beacon. The waters of the River Severn raged in a way I had not previously seen. Peering into the murk, forcing my eyes to adjust to the estuary like a fixed-focal-length lens, I watched grey waves rise and fall as if they were leviathans lunging at low-flying gulls. Furious winds whipped silver spray into swirls, like dust devils in the desert. The wind beat hard at the body of the car. It was at this moment, I think, that I first appreciated the volatility and indifference, the aggression, of the natural world. I longed to touch it. I wound down the window and let cold air and rain gush in. My parents began to shout and my brother's face turned ugly, grotesque: "What the *hell* are you doing?"

I felt something enter, something sinister. My sense of security, my very sense of the world, was compromised; things were changing and my chronic fear of sleep rose to the surface.

We drove further into the night, passing two cities and evading the valleys, before emerging from the darkness onto a bright dual carriageway. We crossed two or three roundabouts—I can't claim to recall with any accuracy the lay of the roads at that time—and hit a strange intersection, where routes from the town met those from the coast. Warehouses, factories and a pub spilled from an adjacent industrial estate—my dad owned an electrical wholesale firm there.

We slipped onto another A-road, passed a new McDonald's and a KFC, and slid into a strip of suburbia separating the town from its surrounding countryside. We drove along the road on which my eldest brother and his wife had recently bought their first house, beneath the hill where the huge secondary school I'd attended for the previous term stood, and across the T-junction onto the street that had been my home since birth. We rolled down the slope, past two of our closest friends' houses and the turning to the cul-de-sac where my grandparents once lived, and arrived finally at ours, plunging into the driveway and activating the security lights. We were not alone.

***

That night, we ate beans on toast and probably watched *Last of the Summer Wine*. Me and my brother played table tennis and PlayStation, our bare feet pressed deep into thick carpet, and the clock ticked on, gathering speed. I observed with dread as the final hour neared. I went to the kitchen to fetch a glass of water, and the sight of the back corridor, gaping like a throat, sent a ripple through my body—an after-effect of another petrifying nightmare. The blind had not been pulled over the window above the sink. I peered at my distorted reflection. Wind howled across the wide expanse of playing fields that stretched from our garden fence right up to the river below Bluebells Wood.

I had never slept with ease, not for as long as I could remember. I had a complicated relationship with the dark and, more profoundly, with silence. From a young age, I'd experienced recurring nightmares of waking up in the fields in the dead of night. I'd see blue flashing lights in our living room, but no matter how hard I ran, the distance would only expand and I'd sink back towards the river winding away to the castles and the coast, squirming with eels and trout. Sometimes I'd see a figure, nebulous, inhuman, crawling from room to room as my parents sat in front of the TV. I'd try to shout but nothing would come. I'd watch paralysed as death drew near, totally silent.

When I couldn't sleep, I'd listen to *Just William* and *Narnia* audio-cassettes, fearing the end of each chapter or story, as that would tell me how long I'd lain awake for and seemed to confirm that I would do so for hours to come. I'd let the tapes click out and then lie in silence, unable to stand any more of time's cruelty. I'd try to imagine nice things, but nothing worked. Knowing that everyone else in the house was asleep was the worst feeling of all—I have never since felt so alone.

If my parents were still up, I would sit at the top of the stairs and cough. Sometimes they'd come with kindness and sympathy, other times exasperation. They could not help me. Nevertheless, I longed for their presence and would beg them to ascend the stairs and kiss me goodnight just once more. When going to bed each evening, having brushed my teeth, I'd expect them both to come and reassure me with a simple peck that I would see them the next day. They generally obliged, unless one of them was out for the evening or the whole night, which was hell. Once they'd left my room, I'd call over and over, "Love you, see you in the morning," until they were out of earshot, or simply chose not to respond. I was reminded emphatically of how all this felt years later, when I read Proust for the first time.

This occasion, however, was different. It wasn't just about sleep and night-time insecurities—it was about the stability of the waking world, the atomic structure of everything and everyone. Nothing would be the same, I could feel it in my bones.

For some reason, it occurred to me that we should go to a supermarket, where it was light and busy and, perhaps, safe. "Shall we go to Tesco?" There was a large Tesco near the KFC and MacDonald's, just out of town, or a smaller one closer in, near the bus station. Alternatively, we could go to Sainsbury's by the new outlet store, next to the motorway junction on the other side of town. I didn't care. "What is *wrong* with you?" my brother replied.

I brushed my teeth in front of the mirror and listened again to the whistling gusts hurtling back and forth over the fields. Rain spattered the bathroom window, double-glazed and iridescent in the glow from the streetlights at the front of the house. I sat on the toilet and shivered. I left the bathroom, passed my brother at the top of the stairs—"*freak*"—and called to Mum and Dad: "I'm going to bed." Ten minutes later, she came into my room. "Goodnight." She kissed me on the cheek and ran her hand through my hair. "See you in the morning." As she descended the stairs, having switched off the main light and turned on a small lamp outside my sister's old room, I called to her. It wasn't a word, but rather a noise—base, primitive and pleading. "Sleep well," she called back and disappeared into the lounge below. He came in after her and said four clinical prayers; he, too, kissed my forehead and left.

Finally, I closed my eyes, faces warped and broken whirling around me, pale breasts oscillating in the dark. Fires began to blaze and the crowns of trees lurched from side to side. The river ran from behind our house up to my bedroom door, seeping underneath; the bones of dead animals somersaulting in the flow, carcasses strewn over the carpet. This was not a dream. For the first and only time in my life, the attic trapdoor in the ceiling outside my room broke and the ladder dropped down with a thud onto the landing. The whole house shook. Like a small child, I longed to flee into my parents' arms, but I chose instead to stay put.

THE BOX OF KNOWLEDGE

I looked across at Dan and felt the anger boil in the pit of my stomach. He'd clung on to the joint for at least five puffs too many, dragging far too hard on the butt, and now it was fucked. Brown tar, the same colour as the stain on his sickly-thin lips, had accumulated at the roach and transformed the thin strip of rolled Rizla packet into an impassable mulch.

"You fuckin' dick," I spat.

He looked at me with stoned eyes, calm and collected, and blew a kiss through the smoke, before returning to the job in hand. He caught hold of the oily mess with his filthy fingernails and tugged it dexterously from between the skins.

"Chill out," he whispered. "I'll sort it."

The box was shrinking and stank from weeks, perhaps even months, of abuse. Our once clean, well-ordered receptacle had fallen into disarray and was no longer ours alone. The floor that Geraint had meticulously swept at the end of each session was now littered with crushed cans of cheap lager and half-bottles of whisky, patches of black ash and sticky booze trampled into the wood. There was a pile of human shit in one corner and the sides of the bin were crusted with old vomit. At least tonight it was just us.

"I want to hurt you so fuckin' much," I muttered under my breath.

"Huh?"

"Nothing." I folded my arms on the table, empty but for pot paraphernalia and a litre bottle of coke filled with fag ends, and pressed my eyes into the crook of my right arm. The walls, sweating a skunky moisture into our atmosphere, leaned in on me and I began to drift.

***

When I was eight, I pulled the legs off a spider. I felt sick with shame afterwards, but at the time I enjoyed it. I was playing with a plastic figurine at the top of the stairs in my parents' house, tying a piece of string around the toy's ankle and hanging it from a banister pole, when the creature, large and angular, stumbled upon our game.

"Oh, hello," I said. "Have you come to play?"

I gave it the role of a bloodthirsty beast and positioned the figurine repeatedly in its path. I used my palms to shape its track as it scuttled left and right, working for a way round. The first amputation was an accident. I'd crawled onto the upstairs landing and was hunched on my hands and knees beside the entrance to the bathroom. The spider, frantic by now, exploited a gap beneath my arched wrist and rushed towards a small crack in the skirting board. Almost mechanically, I pressed my finger down on its left side, indiscriminate and without any real malice, and managed by fluke to pin its back leg to the carpet, roughly at the point where the femur meets the patella. The limb came loose with only the slightest hint of resistance, within which I felt the strangest surge of pleasure. It was so delicate an act and yet so catastrophically destructive.

    I continued in this vein for the next ten minutes or so. I'd left one leg at the foot of the toilet, three by the wicker washing basket and two more beneath the cabinet—in which my parents stored toilet rolls and anti-dandruff shampoo—when my mother intervened. She came in with an armful of towels and immediately registered the sorry specimen squirming beneath me on the linoleum floor. Despite always claiming that the erratic motion of the spindly legs working in tandem was responsible for her crippling fear of arachnids, she screamed louder than I had ever heard before.

"What the hell are you doing? Get back now—get away from it!"

The realisation was instant and, throwing myself hard against the shower screen, I began to cry.

"I'm sorry," I sobbed. "I'm so sorry." For the first time in my life, as far as I can remember, my mother refused to take me into her arms. Instead she turned away, covering her mouth, and left me to my guilt.

Since then, I've anguished long and hard over my capacity for cruelty. It remains a mystery to me. I've become adept at resisting the temptation, albeit occasional, to inflict physical harm. Once or twice, however, the impulse has been so sudden and overwhelming that I've shocked those around me with flashes of my inner violence, but the consequences have usually been minor. Never again, I promised myself that day, would I commit to my urges with such ruinous abandon.

***

Geraint knocked for me at noon and we set off for Spar Lane to meet Dan and Az. It was spring and the sun loomed low over the town, suspended between two vast bulges of grey cumulonimbus. White windfarms spun and shone on the surrounding hilltops, swaying amid broken beams of light as if to the rhythm of an old folk ritual. As we skated past the medieval church overlooking the dual carriageway, a murder of crows erupted from the roof of a derelict bingo hall in the distance. The birds shifted, like starlings, into the shape of a barrelling wave, before executing a perfect human profile, petrified and almost certainly deceased. The natural world had been showing me such things for over a year now, but since the incident with the waterfall on the school trip in the valley, I'd decided to keep quiet.

"Alright, boys? About time, like," said Az, tapping a blue disposable against the stone wall behind, and then proceeding to light his cigarette. "Good last night, weren't it?"

The previous evening, kids we knew from across the borough—from the town centre and its suburbs, from two large housing estates, a web of country lanes and dozens of outlying farms—came together at the local football club to drink, take drugs and listen to hardcore punk music. There was something of a do-it-yourself scene thriving in the area, which gave purpose and community to those of us otherwise at a loose end. Such nights unified the skaters, smokers, drifters and deviants, and anyone else at all bored of or resistant to the expected trajectory, which consisted mainly of a dedication to sport and complete adherence to the word of church, school and state. That's how we saw it, anyway.

"Yeah, was alright," I said, throwing a quick glance at Dan, who was staring down the lane at a bloke sitting on the kerb next to the bus stop. "Weird, though. And my head's fucking killing me. What do you reckon—is it still there?"

"Only one way to find out."

The clubhouse, as always, had been full and hot. We'd arrived just as the penultimate act was finishing its sound-check, so Az and I worked our way into the mass clambering for the bar, while Dan and Geraint tagged on to a table of lads from the year above. We'd already drunk a couple of bottles of Mad Dog at the bend in the river, next to the circle of phony standing stones in the park, and I was feeling pretty good. Every familiar face, nodding and smiling, added to my growing sense that tonight was sure to be a good one. I longed to get stuck into deep, drunken conversation and the chaos of the pit. I was also on the lookout for Katie, who, Anna had told me the day before, wanted to get to know me better.

"What you havin'?" asked Az. "Pint?"

"Yeah—let's have a shot as well." We showed our fake ID cards and bought four pints of watery lager, knocked back a shot of tequila each and made our way across to the others.

Weaving through the crowds of wild-haired, tattooed teenagers in baggy skate clothes, avoiding the clutter of upturned chairs and piles of smashed glass, I marvelled at my confidence. For so long I'd been on the periphery, incapable of contributing to locker-room banter, failing miserably at masculine small talk and thus never really belonging, whatever that means. Instead of persisting with a project of supposed self-improvement, I began to accept and embrace my position on the edge. It was there I came to know others like myself: suspicious of order, sick of repetition, longing for difference. Every day after school, we'd flee from our family homes into the surrounding landscape, claiming strips of forgotten woodland and frequenting neglected backstreets, alleyways and broken-down buildings. We found solace beneath bridges, in factory car parks and beside railway tracks. Immersed in the freedom these places could afford, I learned to talk openly and without restraint, and people seemed to like what I had to say. Now here I was, striding through the ghost of an old welfare hall, inhaling the glorious, fruity stench of disorder, pissed up with friends and basking in the admiration of a beautiful girl.

"Cheers, boys." Dan and Geraint nodded their appreciation as we placed their drinks in front of them, sloshing large sips of lager onto the graffitied wood. I sat down on a bench against the wall—noting how similar the floral pattern was to that of my grandparents' upholstery—squeezing between Joe, who worked on the checkout at Tesco, and Craig, who I'd played football with a few years back. Both were pale as milk, hunched over and silent, with their heads propped on their hands. Less than optimistic about the chance of a decent chat, I wriggled the pouch of tobacco from my jeans and began to roll a cigarette.

"Put some of this in if you want, boy," said Craig, unfolding himself from his stupor. He pulled back the waist on his trousers, reached down towards his crotch and withdrew a small plastic bag bulging with buds of lime-green skunk.

"Thanks, man." I picked off a series of pea-sized lumps and crumbled them like pieces of dried soil into the roll-up splayed open on my lap. It always pleased me, the way the grass seemed to fluff out and grow in quantity, as if by magic.

There was never any real worry of getting caught smoking pot in gigs like this. The atmosphere was typically dense with smoke, and as long as you could roll a joint fairly discretely, resisting the temptation to use more than one skin, you'd be fine. Just act like you were smoking a fag and if security came too close, drop it on the floor, step on it and kick it away—simple as that.

While the band launched into their opening track, I lit up, pulled hard on the roach a few times, inhaled deeply and blew two ribbons of smoke from my nose, before passing the joint to Craig, who passed it quickly on to Joe and then Az. We continued this way for the whole set, getting more and more stoned, stopping only to fetch another four pints. It seemed to go like this with our extended group of friends: a small gesture, such as sharing your weed, would bond you for the rest of the night and, sometimes, for months to come. I loved the ease and spontaneity with which we'd slip into new relationships.

During the interim, we bought Joe and Craig a shot each and in turn they suggested we join them in the stand opposite the clubhouse for something too risky to be done indoors.

As we left the table, I felt Dan's jealous gaze burn the back of my neck, but fuck him—he'd been pissing me off all week. I did a brief scan of the room for Katie, but could see neither her, nor any of her friends, which was probably a good thing, considering how stoned I was. We pushed through the crowd gathered at the entrance and walked out onto the dark football pitch, leapfrogging the railings and trampling over the sopping turf. The centre circle was totally waterlogged from the deluge earlier in the day. As we neared the stand—engulfed in shadow, gaping like a wound in the night—I heard voices and laughter, the flicker of lighter flames flashing still images of people we probably knew. A familiar excitement flowed through my body.

"This way," Joe called, having set his course for the furthest corner, behind which was a wall separating the ground from the club's narrow car park. We sat down on the cold concrete and Craig took from his wallet a small, folded wrap of paper that looked like a page torn from a porno magazine.

"Ever done speed before, boys?"

Az nodded: "A couple of times, yeah." I'd smoked some in a joint once, but I shook my head.

"Best thing for gigs, like—gets the music right inside you. And you'll have no bother talking to the girls."

He scooped a miniature heap of the pinkish powder onto the end of his moped key and snorted it back. Joe and Az did the same, and I followed suit. The effect was immediate: the cold air felt suddenly comforting, like the cool side of the pillow on a hot night; the cigarette I'd sparked up twenty seconds earlier became as essential to me as oxygen or water; and the distant clatter of drums and the twang of tuning guitars filled me with a seething energy.

"Az, is that you?"

We turned around to see Anna, Katie and two or three others shuffling down the raised top step towards us. This was perfect—I felt fantastic. For the next twenty minutes, we shared their spliffs, drank from a flagon of cider and talked about the bands we were currently listening to. This was a discussion I was keen to lead, expert as I was in the field of punk music past and present—it was my thing. I talked and talked, slurring and spitting, interrupting and elaborating on others' points. Geraint and Dan appeared from nowhere and the latter watched me with a self-satisfied smile. As I delved into the poetic merits of early Bad Religion, I caught a look passed between Anna and Katie that I couldn't quite comprehend. I decided to slow down and let the others speak, realising, too, that I was desperate to pee.

I was about to unleash onto a square sheet of corrugated iron, when I noticed I was directly behind where the group were sitting. I moved, instead, to a patch of wall to the right, over the top of which I could see into the car park. As I soaked the brickwork with figures of eight, a loud crash reverberated through the floor, making me spray my jeans as I stuffed my shrunken penis back into my pants. Through the darkness, I could just about register the outline of a large red box. A container, perhaps? It was elevated on some sort of trailer.

"Shit!" A second noise plunged my nerves into havoc. I flung myself down into a crouching position, so that I was well hidden, and peered over the wall. From the far side of the container—which, as my eyes adjusted, I recognised as the rear compartment of an Eddie Stobart lorry—a figure lurched, bent and limping, towards the trees bordering a patch of industrial wasteland. Just as the figure was about to disappear into the foliage, it dropped onto all fours and scrambled away, grunting like a hog.

"What the fuck are you doin'?" Az laughed. He and Geraint were walking towards me. "That whiz fuckin' you up is it, boy?"

I placed my finger on my lips and waved them over.

"Something weird's going on," I explained. I was reluctant to describe the creature I'd seen, in case my mind was playing tricks, but the unlikely geography of this alien object alone was worth investigating.

"It might be a drugs stash," Geraint suggested, hopefully.

We crept around the unit to the back doors, my heart thumping rapidly from the combination of whiz, booze and terror. Despite what I'd seen, though, I was enjoying the sensation of the wet gravel crunching beneath my feet. I loved this sort of thing: fear, exhilaration, disordered senses. I reached for the bolt rusting inside the barrel of the sliding lock and placed my palm flat into a blob of slime. I paused to let my eyes focus properly on the red liquid dripping from my fingers to my wrist.

"What the fuck!" I vaulted backwards with my hand raised to show the others.

Geraint started: "What's wrong, what happened?"

I rotated the affected limb one way and then the other, stunned to find it now dry, the red goo vanished.

"Nothing," I said. "I caught my finger."

I pulled the door wide open, pushed myself up on the steel step, and came to rest on my knees in a sort of porch area. I lifted my head to see a second, wooden door, unusually small and with a tiny brass knob on one side. The boys joined me on the platform and Az leaned forward, barely touching the handle before the door clicked and swung inwards with a whine. I bowed into the room and felt a musky blast rush immediately up my nostrils. The rotten stench carried images of dead animals: a hedgehog slit open in the garden; a rabbit, mauled and bloody, bathing in its own mush; a squirrel squashed on the sizzling road, surrounded by a tragic spillage of nuts; and, of course, a spider squirming on the bathroom floor.

Geraint tugged cautiously on a cord hanging above his head and with a *tick*, a precise arrangement popped into view. Beneath a blackened bulb, which cast out a dim red light, stood a table with an empty bowl on top—a crust of cold soup, perhaps, drying on the porcelain edge. A camping bed, neatly made, was positioned with geometric perfection against the back panelling, and a stack of four plastic chairs arched forward from the far corner. There was also a small collection of pots and pans in a cardboard box, a portable gas cooker and a pile of science fiction books swollen with damp. On the floor, beneath the table, was a moth-eaten rug—beige and purple, peppered with morsels of mouldy food. The reek of decay was at war with the somewhat pleasing aroma of stale cigarettes.

"Fuckin' hell, this is proper creepy." Geraint's face was ashen; he was trying to rid himself of a cobweb clinging to the tips of his gelled hair.

"Jesus!" From the direction of the deserted brownfield site came a howl of such intensity that my legs buckled and I threw my arms up to protect my face. Az and Geraint both dropped a foot or so, as if their feet had been sliced off at the ankles. We looked from one another to the table, the bed and the empty coat hook by the door, then leapt into action, clawing to get out. We jumped down onto the gravel, hurdled the bricks and railings, and stumbled onto the football pitch.

As we fled towards the safety of the clubhouse—lights blinking in the meshed windows, the tinny sound of the last band starting to play—Geraint strayed into the centre circle; he slipped five feet into the air, his body whipping parallel to the ground, and dropped into a pool of mud and rainwater. In an instant, our fear dissipated and we burst into fits of hysterical laughter. A crowd of silhouettes just yards ahead turned and, as soon as they saw the drenched figure emerging from the swamp, joined in our delirium. As they approached for a closer look, I caught a glimpse of Dan doubled over coughing, pulling his hand loose from Katie's.

***

"I know him," Geraint said, pointing at the body slumped next to the bus stop as we exited the lane and crossed the road by Spar. "Used to drink in the Shoes with my brothers. It's depressing seeing him like that."

Brimming with the thrill of our new discovery, we set off to retrace our steps. We passed a mustard-coloured pub, its paint and plaster crumbling like pastry, and approached the chip shop where Az used to work, before he got caught with his fingers in the till. We turned right, walked half a mile or so along the main road and then branched off down a narrow footpath, between a row of semi-detached houses and a cluster of overgrown allotments. My vision was fading in and out of focus and my stomach writhed, still struggling to make sense the previous night's chemicals.

A beam of sunlight bounced off a collapsed greenhouse, drawing our attention to a broad old man in a check shirt and brown sleeveless pullover—someone's grandfather, I seemed to recall. He greeted us from his chair, tilting a can of cider towards us and winking enthusiastically, cheeks ablaze.

"Hiya," we called, avoiding eye-contact.

I looked north into the sky and found the moon, a spectral trace, or imprint, of its usual self. The sun had emerged from between the clouds and the morning's grey pallor was almost gone, replaced by a blend of crisp cobalt blue and tentative streams of yellow heat.

Just on from the vegetable plots, a sequence of boulders marked the threshold separating the industrial tract—into which the creature had fled—from civilisation. We knew this spot well. At its core was a small portacabin, disused and disintegrating, around which revolved a medley of black bags and plastic crates, shopping trolleys and patches of scorched concrete. An abandoned railway line ran along the far side, and a banking sloped away towards a large power station on the left, pylons stretching into the ether like huge silver trees. Furnished with rotund tufts of couch grass and coils of thick bramble, this was a terrain for wayfarers, pot smokers and fly tippers. To the right was the slice of woodland backing onto the football club.

"Let's cut through," said Az, with a grin, as he lit another cigarette.

Rambling across this post-apocalyptic landscape, I felt both at home and astray, swimming in some strange but comforting liquid realm. This was part of the appeal: a place to challenge and unsettle; to explore and be explored; to facilitate, embrace and share. It was a site to claim, fleetingly, but not own. It was the sort of setting where structure and expectations fell away, time slowed and there was room enough to breathe. Metaphor and poetry became real. We could run our young engines ragged and then rest and recuperate, free from prying eyes. We could destroy and rebuild. For brief periods we could be ourselves, or at least have a good fumble with the idea of who we were.

"Oh, Jesus—fucking hell." Dan had his hands on his hips and was looking in the direction of the wood.

I caught sight of a tangle of bodies, brown and feathered, tumbling in the grit and soil beneath the skeleton of a juvenile field maple—a decades-old monument to one of the local authority's failed planting schemes. We came to within fifteen feet and stood in total silence, watching a buzzard pin a woodpigeon to the earth, peck its eyes and then hop a yard or two away, before repeating. The pigeon flapped and squealed frantically for bursts of about ten seconds and then collapsed in an exhausted heap, scratching and bleeding into the dried mud. Its body was covered in yawning wounds, pieces of tooth-white bone glistening amid shredded flesh.

"That's disgusting," Geraint said. "Come on, let's go."

While the others walked on, I remained transfixed, watching this magnificent predator plunge its talons into the breast of its prey, an exquisite crushing of bone and cartilage, the heart punctured. I visualised deep-red fluid leaking and pooling in the body's various crevices, organs spasming towards death. I loved raptors—prehistorically wild, far beyond any language of mine. As if with sudden respect, the buzzard took its meal in a tender grip and dragged it half a metre along the floor, before arching its wings and pulling itself into the air, a runnel of dust pirouetting in its wake. I ran to catch up with the boys.

"It's still there," Az called, brushing a knot of twigs from his face and navigating a path out of a shallow ditch. Beyond a screen of overhanging branches, we could see the red box, perched neatly in a section of shade at the back of the car park, deceptively dull-looking.

We hammered bravely, with clenched fists, against the heavy-duty steel and waited for a response: nothing. We climbed in through the double doors, just as before, and came upon the same meticulous arrangement, unchanged down to the finest detail: the books, the bowl, the crust of soup.

"I see what you mean," Dan said, nodding, taking it all in. He clapped his hands together and smiled: "Let's roll a joint."

The climate was close and claustrophobic, a fuggy miasma swirling throughout. We flung open the rear portal and let the cool breeze pour in. Geraint fetched the chairs stacked in the corner and positioned them around the table, while I leafed through the novels piled against a poorly-assembled chest of drawers: old Badger prints authored by obscure pseudonyms—Victor La Salle, Bron Fane, Karl Zeigfreid and Erle Barton, among others. The last volume in the collection was *The Watching World*, by Lionel Fanthorpe; it couldn't be the same Lionel Fanthorpe as my media studies teacher, could it? How many Lionel Fanthorpe's were there? This was bizarre.

Satisfied with our attempt at ventilation, we slammed the doors, shutting ourselves away from the currents and routines of the town. Az emptied his rucksack: tobacco, skins, a homemade bong, countless packets of junk food. We took our seats, passed around small bags of mind-obliterating super skunk and settled into the familiar rituals of rolling and toasting, chatting shit and taking the piss. Through a thickening veil of sinister grey vapour, I watched Dan laugh and joke as he recalled his violent antics in the midst of last night's mosh pit. He paused to focus on shaping the end of his spliff into a cone, his lips in the motion of silent speech, talking himself through it. Without knowing how or why, I slid into a fantasy of turning him over on a mountain of slag, slashing at his bulbous brown eyes with sharpened nails, pushing his skull hard into the ground. I arched my back, breathed in the aroma of fresh meat and sinew, and prepared to take flight.

***

For the next however many weeks, we returned regularly to what spontaneously became known as the Box of Knowledge. Usually, we'd arrange to meet at the car park as soon as possible after school, and on weekends we'd set off first thing, often spending entire days drifting in our cramped oblivion. Whoever, or whatever, it was that deserted their dwelling that first evening gave no indication of coming back, so we soon relaxed; Az took the bowl and spoon outside and threw them into the bushes.

Geraint made it his business to see to the general upkeep of the receptacle. He ran a tight ship, demanding shoes off in the porch, systematic airings and almost-daily wipe downs—he arrived one morning with a broom from his parents' utility closet and for a significant spell swept with surprising diligence. He stopped only about the time he started complaining of double vision and a persistent pain in his knee.

During this period, my burgeoning ill feeling towards Dan grew more and more intense. I came to despise the slow pace at which he seemed to move through life, which was exacerbated by the curious stiffness he was now experiencing in his joints. This, coupled with the idiosyncratic animations of his ludicrous face, which conveyed only either concentration or sly amusement, was enough to set my teeth to grinding. One evening, he brought Anna and Katie along, flirting mercilessly and, according to him, effectively, despite the fact he was becoming somewhat repetitious in conversation. We all were.

I sat for at least an hour watching him chat away, joking and drumming on his knees to the beat of Geraint's battery-powered cassette player. Between my legs, I rotated the point of my father's razor-sharp angling knife repeatedly on my knuckle, drawing small globules of blood onto the blade, and then began chipping sizeable splints from the table. Now and then I would jerk the whole thing hard to the right, so that everyone turned to look at me, confused and irritated. Katie appeared repulsed. A few days later, when Dan pushed his way in through the door, I used a can of deodorant and a Clipper lighter to launch a torrent of fire into his face. He fell over onto his side and then rose swiftly, taking me by the collar of my shirt and slamming me into the wall, the stench of singed hair filling the compartment. From their seats, Az and Geraint laughed like hyenas. For the most part, though, we'd try to remain civil.

Soon enough, others discovered our hideout and a competition ensued as to who could get in first, so as to claim the best chairs. Too often, we'd find ourselves reduced to squeezing together on the bed, or, worse, the floor. What's more, the kids responsible, who were generally older and commanded respect and admiration, proved unpredictable and bullyish. It was one of them, I was positive, who did the shit in the corner, not that any fucker would own up to it.

With our sense of order and responsibility diminished, the Box of Knowledge descended into squalor. We spilt drinks, spat, flicked ash aimlessly and threw scraps of food at one another. Our clay-caked shoes remained on our feet and the once regular airings became few and far between. Geraint took to placing sheets of newspaper stolen from outside Spar over the piles of vomit (and, of course, faeces) that sporadically appeared. One morning, upon entering, we were confronted by a dead rabbit sprawled and gutted on the floor, the reek of warm animal carcass, so familiar from childhood, intermingling with the heavy effluvia of adolescence. We simply flicked it outside with a stick, before settling in to prepare a mix for another extended session on the bong.

***

I lifted my head from my arms and looked across at him again: his fumbling hands, a trickle of saliva dangling from his almost non-existent lower lip. I noticed creases crawling away from his eyes, reaching towards his thinning hairline. He seemed older.

"Told you I'd sort it," he whispered, slotting in the new roach and flinging the lit joint in my direction. It spun into my chest and burst into a spray of glowing embers, like a tiny firework.

"You fucking dick!" I grabbed the Coke bottle by the cap end and hurled it straight at Dan's head. He ducked just in time to avoid the missile, but it exploded against the wall behind, showering his back with fag butts and a crude yellow liquid. He jumped to his feet, tipping his chair over.

"What the fuck is wrong with you?"

I curled my fingers instinctively around the fishing knife throbbing in my pocket.

"Jesus. Chill out boys." Geraint's gravelly voice floated between us. "You're freakin' me out."

Az laughed: "Leave 'em to it, boy—we'll have a full-on fight to watch soon." From a lazy slouch, he blew a succession of smoke hoops into the air. "Who's your money on?" Geraint shook his head and ignored the question.

Dan twisted his body awkwardly, wiping the froth from his coat, and heaved an exasperated sigh. As he stooped to pick up his chair, I released the weapon from my grip and took a long swig of flat, flavourless lager from the can in front of me. I began to feel stupid.

We'd arrived just as the sun was dipping below the silhouette of an estate on one of the surrounding hills. We'd told our parents we were staying at each other's houses, when in fact we planned to spend the whole night camped in the box, drinking and getting stoned. Everyone else we hung out with would be at the recreation centre, watching a band who had travelled west from the capital. There was a house party, too, which meant we would not be disturbed. It wasn't like us to miss such events, but we'd grown cynical and insecure in our isolation. We convinced ourselves we were disillusioned by the superficiality of the scene, despite all it had done for us. And, anyway, we had better music on the cassette player.

"Time for shots then, boyos." Az poured four large measures of whisky into a row of tumblers and proceeded to drop a small, pink tablet into each. We downed the concoction, cranked up the volume and waited for our bodies to change.

Outside, a storm descended on the town. Heavy winds clattered through the streets, baying like hounds on the Wild Hunt. Gallons of rain sloshed over kerbs into driveways and flowerbeds, drowning all manner of domestic plant life. Children, rushed indoors by feverish parents, traipsed sewage and other detritus over thick, well-nourished rugs and carpets. The river burst its banks, flooding the playing fields with gunk and eels, rats and the bones of lost pets. Two trees came down that night, one of which crushed a white van, the other blocked the road up to the school. We listened to the raging weather pelt our capsule and tear at the outer canvas, as if to get in.

Soon enough, time shirked its rhythm and my friends' faces grew gaunt and obscure in the haze. I lost the ability to think in a linear flow, instead letting words and images, movements and emotions, flash like a broken film reel before me. I saw my parents, grandparents, brothers and sisters reflected in shards of glass. I saw dead animals hanging on a clothes line, and a plastic wrestling figure entwined in ribbons of silk. The backs of my hands, when I turned them over, were covered in what looked like liver spots. There was someone on the bed, rubbing and slithering in the murk. An enormous spider inched sideways towards me from the corner of the room; I gathered my legs into my arms.

At some point, the rapid beat of the blaring music drew us from our seats. We flung ourselves forwards and backwards, colliding and crashing hard, burying our knees into one another's hips and torsos. Alternate blasts of fury and euphoria washed over us in waves. Amid the booze and the bodies—more by the minute, it seemed—I could feel Dan's malicious stare, stalking me through the melee.

I came to on the floor, my shoulders slumped against the bed-frame and my legs outstretched in front of me. Most of the smoke had cleared, leaving behind a familiar, rich odour. I scanned the box, struggling to bring its component parts into focus. My head was pounding and a deep sense of dread began to stir within me.

The last thing I could clearly recall was throwing a bottle of Coke at Dan and then drinking a shot of something sinister. I coughed hard and looked at the table, at Geraint asleep face down on the wood. A vision rose of figures dancing around me, Dan's features twisted and grimacing in the dark. I turned to the right and waited while the scene of chaos and destruction eased away its blurred edges: broken furniture, piles of cans and upturned ashtrays. Small streaks of what looked like blood were smeared over some of the panels. To the left, I found Az unconscious on the mattress, curled inside his sleeping bag. Where was Dan? Another memory emerged, formless but infused with wrath. A piercing squeal echoed at the rear of my skull. I felt in my pocket for the knife; it was gone.

I rose quickly and stumbled unsteadily around the box, knocking anything that was still standing to the ground. My cheekbones ached and my lips were split and stinging. I pinched at the dried fluid on my knuckles, panic churning my guts to pulp. At the back of our vessel, I came upon an irregular stack of something covered in sheets of newspaper and random items of clothing. There was a pool of blood at its base. As if in a nightmare, I bent down and lifted the first page to reveal a damp, worn-out combat boot. In a sudden mania, I tore the rest of the concealment away, exposing a body like nothing I had ever seen: somehow miniature, like a child, but with the face of a man crossed with a hog, or some other wild creature. Its shoulders were severely hunched and the cranium appeared to have been caved in by a major blunt force trauma. Protruding from the middle of its chest was my father's angling knife.

    I turned around and walked calmly back to my spot by the bed, telling myself it was all a dream. I sat down and rolled a cigarette, which I proceeded to smoke with my eyes closed. I longed, with every fibre of my being, to return home to my family, to lie on the sofa and be soothed by my mother's voice. I slid onto my side and slipped away.

***

When I awoke, the sky was clear and blue, and I could hear the sound of a match taking place nearby. Dan was prodding Geraint in the chin with a stick, cooing and laughing. A shiver rippled through my body and I lifted myself from the dew-sodden turf. I stretched my arms and back, my distorted spine clicking into order, and shook Dan's hand. I glanced around and recognised where we were as the patch of grass next to the football club car park. The others rose and we walked together to the place where the Box of Knowledge had stood ever since that first night. Nothing remained but for a series of depressions in the gravel and clay. I examined my hands, the skin deceptively fresh and taut, at odds with the person I had become, and then zipped my coat.

"So that's the end of that," Az remarked with a smirk, lighting another cigarette. He handed it to Dan, who took two puffs, before passing it on to me. With the windmills turning in the distance, birdsong sizzling in the trees, we set off in search of somewhere new—somewhere else into which, for a time, we could disappear.

AN ORKNEY SAGA

One summer, my father took us, Rob and I, to the Orkney Islands, to see the Viking burial sites, Pictish and Neolithic ruins, and to do some fishing. I was still in primary school—year five, I think. The first evening we arrived, we watched three locals unload their catch from a small motorboat onto the boggy shore of the lake we were staying on. We ate dinner in a barn, or outbuilding, with stuffed fish mounted on the walls, gawping over our shoulders at our food. Dad drank Guinness, as he would each night for the coming week, while me and my brother sipped ice-cold cans of Irn-Bru. I don't remember what we spoke about, just that Rob kept repeating Will Smith's line from *Independence Day*: "Let's kick the tires and light the fires, Big Daddy."

We fished most mornings, Dad steering us out to the silky deep, but didn't catch a thing. He'd choose a spot, kill the engine and cast our lines, then wait quietly for a bite. Every so often, one of our wires got snagged in the weeds. My lack of experience meant the first few times this happened, I flicked my rod and shouted, "I've got something," only to reel in handfuls of mulch. After every twenty minutes or so—not nearly long enough—Dad broke the silence by announcing we were to move on, because the fish were surely basking in that pool of sun over there, or whatever. Reflecting on our failure one night, he blamed the seal apparently stalking the boat and stealing our trout.

    We'd travelled to Scotland a number of times before our week in Orkney. I'm not sure how many trips we'd made, but they've all sort of amalgamated into one in my mind. I recall, for instance, a murder of crows alighting on the roof of Edinburgh Castle, and that very same day, as far as I can tell, driving beside Loch Ness. I was obsessed with the monster mythology and told everyone I was going to see it. And then I did. I had this pamphlet with a condensed history of the beast—a few grainy black and white shots dispersed between paragraphs—that I must have read a thousand times or more. I loved the 'Surgeon's Photograph'—categorical proof, if any was needed, that some time-evading horror lurked below us and would, on occasion, rise to the surface.

    I held on tight to this leaflet as we drove along a narrow country road. There was a screen of lush green foliage to my left, beyond which the water bobbed and chopped. I longed for a breach, and sure enough it came. I'd only been looking at the loch for a matter of minutes—ten perhaps, without averting my eyes—when two humps broke the crest of a wave, followed by a third and fourth, and finally the pointed tail, the last bit to disappear back into the sloshing abyss. It was over in three seconds flat, only ripples remaining, working away from the site of incision like lights on a radar dial.

"There—I saw it! Look, over there! Look at the water!"

My parents were enjoying my burgeoning interest in cryptozoology and had told me they, too, believed in the creature.

"Well, there you go," Mum said, "you've seen it now. You can tell Nan when we get back to the hotel."

"Did you see it, though?" I was bouncing in my seat.

They smiled at each other and Dad confirmed he had, indeed, seen something.

Nearing the end of our time in Orkney, we visited Maeshowe, a Neolithic cairn and passage grave constructed around 3000 BC. From the outside, it looked like a small hill, a place a hobbit might inhabit. The entrance tunnel, which runs to the central chamber, is only three feet tall, so we had to shuffle through on our hands and knees. As I crawled along, I was struck by the smell of the damp earth, far stronger than that I was familiar with. It left an almost bitter aftertaste. We'd been told there were bodies here and I could feel them. I paused in the passageway, unsure as to whether or not I should go any further, but Rob was gaining on me, so I had to keep moving. It was as if I was being sucked into the ground.

Stepping into the chamber was like stepping out of our world and into a different dimension, a time capsule. While the guide talked about dates and architecture, man-hours and angled buttresses, I zoned out and heard sounds and voices swirling in a maelstrom around me. I'd been thinking a lot, at night, about death and heaven. Dad tried to comfort me with words of God and eternal life, but to be honest the idea of forever scared me more than anything else. I couldn't get my head around it.

I stood facing the wall, looking at an image of a dragon scratched into stone by a Norse graffiti artist in the twelfth century. As recounted in the Orkneyinga Saga, a group of Viking travellers broke into the tomb and left more than thirty runic inscriptions, the world's largest collection of such engravings. It occurred to me that this dragon I was staring at might, in fact, be skulking in the depths of Loch Ness. Had they seen him too?

I flinched at something wet and warm moving along the back of my skull. I turned around to see Rob grinning. He'd taken, lately, to surreptitiously chewing a tuft of hair protruding from my crown—he loved that I hated it so much. "What's the matter with you?"

Back outside, in the fresh air, we walked along the coast. It could have been a different day, I don't know. We paused by a farmer's field and watched a woman delivering a foal, her arm inserted deep inside the back end of the horse. Rob touched the fence and jolted backwards.

"It's electric." He touched it again. "Whoa. That's so weird." He turned to me. "You have a go." I placed my finger on the wire. "Shit!" It felt as though my bones were being pulled from their sockets.

Dad caught up and joined us.

"It's an electric fence," I explained.

"Don't be silly."

The woman in the field looked up. "It is actually. I wouldn't touch it if I were you."

His hands were already stretched out—it was too late to retract them. "Strewth! Bloody hell." The woman shook her head.

We continued walking along the cliffs. The wind was blowing hard now and the sea writhed like a snake pit. Always full of energy, Rob ran on, sidestepping knots of marram grass, skipping over divots and molehills. He was straying dangerously close to the edge.

"Robert, get away from there." Dad was holding my wrist ten or fifteen metres inland. "Come back here with us. The wind is very strong." Rob strolled over, his mouth twisted into a smile.

"What would you do if I fell?"

"I'd grab your brother and jump off too." The words startled me—I looked up to see if he was joking, but his face was stern, almost angry. "I could never go back to *her* with just one." Where was she, anyway? Why hadn't she come with us? I looked out at the ocean, at the thrashing waves, and felt unsafe.

NIGHTS AT THE FACTORY

A cloak of blue darkness swept over the landscape, giving it an abstract character, like an oil painting. I crouched down within a cluster of dustbins, bullets of rain pelting my hood. Geraint, who was stooped with his hands on his knees, coughed loudly.

"Shut the fuck up," Dan hissed, peering around the corner of one of the outbuildings ten yards ahead, watching for the caretaker on his patrol of the factory. Az, who was slouched next to Dan with his back against the wall, lit a cigarette, despite the weather. He cupped his hands over the flame and grinned widely through the pluming smoke.

The factory consisted of a series of beige portacabins, two huge buildings for manufacturing and a monstrous, hangar-like warehouse, which obliterated all sense of proportion. Nearby was the caretaker's shed, anachronistic in its country-village style. The whole plot was spread over four acres situated at the heart of an industrial estate, just off a quiet through road. Opposite was a car park, surrounded by tall hedging—ideal for smoking weed. It was from there we first ventured across to the site, entering through a breach in the steel fence, where the concrete below was cracked and broken, giving way onto a layer of unnaturally coarse soil.

"Don't move, boys." Dan turned to look at us. "He's coming."

The caretaker emerged on the path beside the shed and paused for a moment. He cut a strange figure, short and crooked, proudly unperturbed by the rain, which had fallen for the duration of this oddly mild winter. He could, we'd learned, materialise anywhere on the grounds without warning, as if from thin air—there was no predicting his whereabouts at any given moment. Tonight, he looked to be on high alert, hands clasped behind his back, his bearded chin and wiry curls protruding from the hood of his waterproof. He took one step forward and rotated a full circle on the spot, surveying the panorama. He was expecting us. At the end of last week, he'd written a message in bold paint on the side of one of the temporary offices, amid scorch marks caused by a bonfire we'd lit using plastic crates. It read: *I'll catch you soon and make you wish you'd never been born. Have a nice a day.* He signed it off with a smiley face.

Once he'd disappeared back in the direction from which he'd come, I rose cautiously and ran on tiptoes between a scattering of water-filled potholes to Dan and Az. My socks were sopping in my trainers. Geraint followed behind, then unzipped his rucksack and pulled out a carton of eggs.

"Ready lads?" Az looked thrilled. He flicked the butt of his cigarette onto the nearest rooftop and took two eggs in one hand and a third in the other. We all followed suit. "Meet you on the steps by the warehouse." He whipped his scarf around his mouth and raced delicately through the dense rain towards the shed. As he veered right, coming to within fifteen yards of the front door, he slowed momentarily and unleashed his three missiles in quick succession onto the target. He struck the porch walls and windows with pinpoint precision, then made off into the wet, whirling darkness.

Dan ghosted along the same track, while me and Geraint brought up the rear. I held the eggs as lightly as possible between my fingers, feeling the slime slosh back and forth inside. As we peppered the hut, the sound of the shells crunching against the slats of wood released a surge of what was becoming a too-familiar kind of sadistic pleasure. I smiled to myself as I broke into a sprint, the cool air filling my ragged lungs, and tore for the warehouse. The ground was littered with industrial debris: piping, pallets and something like an engine—a revolting twist of spokes and cylinders rusting in the perpetually damp atmosphere, a monument to these times of change.

Just as I rounded the corner, I heard Geraint yell at the top of his voice—a shrill scream, so unlike him. I glanced back and saw the caretaker haring behind, hot on our heels, his hammer swinging to the rhythm of his strides like a relay baton. My heart pounding, I took a right and skirted the first of the manufacturing buildings. I arrived at a barren space, a blank sprawl of concrete sloped towards a vast rolling shutter—perhaps a loading bay. In the near distance, through the silvery murk, I saw the outer fence, enmeshed with coils of bramble and copper barbed wire. A current of mist spiralled from a row of diseased conifers on the edge of the bordering woodland. Cluttered together next to the loading platform, in the shadows cast by the trees, were at least twenty stainless-steel barrels. I weaved my way through, ignoring the rank stench, and slipped into the alley behind. Sounds from the adjacent woods were suddenly interrupted by those of rushing footsteps and panting breath. I froze, watching the gap at the end of the lane, something bird-like flapping in my chest. A person lurched into view.

The silhouette bent forward and wheezed: "Fuckin' hell." It was Az. He put a cigarette in his mouth and held it over the flame of his Clipper lighter until the tobacco crackled.

I called in a loud whisper: "You okay?"

"Jesus Christ." His body convulsed. "You scared the shit out of me. Come here." He gave me a cigarette and took his phone from his pocket to read a text message. "Dan's on the steps behind the warehouse. Where's Ger?" He was still smiling. He loved this sort of thing.

"Dunno. Lost him back there by the shed—I came down here and he went towards the road. I think the caretaker followed. He was proper close behind."

"Fuckin' hell." He blew smoke in my face. "Did you hear Ger's scream, though? Funny as fuck." His eyes were sparkling. I couldn't help but laugh.

We slid furtively between the buildings to where Dan was waiting. There was no sign of the caretaker, but we kept a cautious eye. We found a patch of dry flagstones below the warehouse eaves and sat with our backs to the brickwork, rolling joints inside our coats. We called Geraint's phone, but it was either out of battery or off the grid.

"He must have gone home," Dan suggested.

"I dunno," I said. "The caretaker was wild tonight. And he was gaining on him fast."

I started to feel seriously worried, not to mention guilty. Should I have stayed with Geraint, instead of increasing my speed when I saw how close the caretaker was? It was a constant struggle, reconciling my preference for flight over fight with the fact that my friends—perhaps disregarding Dan—would do anything for me; I was sure that both Az and Geraint would take hammer blows to the head before leaving me to face the caretaker on my own. I longed for the courage to stand my ground and have their backs, too, but it was simply out of my control: I was a runner, a fact of life that weighed heavy on me, especially in the early hours of the morning, alone in my room.

"And you kept going?" Dan was the only one who'd hold me to account for this weakness. My face flushed with blood and I cowered over the joint splayed open in my lap. I burnt the end of the resin bar and sprinkled pot into the brown slug of tobacco, my shame temporarily assuaged by the sensation of skin blistering on my thumb.

"Don't worry, lad," said Az. "I'd have done the same. None of us expected anyone to get caught."

We huddled together in a tight circle and smoked our spliffs, trying again and again to get hold of our lost friend. The wind picked up and hurtled back and forth across the site like a bull, ricocheting off walls and clattering recklessly into doors and shutters, a chorus of metallic song echoing through the maze. We finished up and made for the gap in the fence, aware of the possibility the caretaker was still stalking us. Relieved to see the line of streetlamps glowing on the empty road, we scrambled through soaked mud and grit to the safety of the pavement on the other side. We shouted Geraint's name back at the factory and waited for a response, but there was none. We chose to walk home via the woods, in case we were being followed; plus, there was a chance we'd bump into Geraint on the way, if he'd made it out. We convinced ourselves he had.

As we strolled between the trees, I looked at the abandoned shopping trolleys, pools of solid plastic melted on the ground and piles of fly-tipped domestic appliances. I felt a tremor rumble beneath my feet. It was as if something massive had slithered below me. The rain, which was now stinging my face, fell heavier again; the leaves around us curled and the branches stretched like limbs. We continued on our way in complete silence.

***

The next morning at school, with the rain still falling, the three of us waited at the top of the steps by the rugby pitch for Geraint to arrive. There was no sign of him. We ignored the bell for registration and after three or four cigarettes, plus a few tracks from the latest Propagandhi album, set off for his house. We walked through town to the estate and stopped at the precinct to buy cans of Coke and packets of crisps, filling our pockets with sweets and chocolate while perusing the shelves.

Outside, the blanket of grey-black cloud dropped even lower, seeming to hang now just metres above the tallest trees, as if night was already encroaching. We crossed a plot of derelict land behind the church and skidded down a bank of gravel, into the strip of wilderness rupturing this otherwise neat zone. The woods, which ran right through the middle of the estate and spread around its entire circumference, were pocked with pillboxes, remnants of the ammunition storage centre built here before the Second World War and concealed by property developers. There were tunnels dug deep into the surrounding terrain, upon which factories, garages and wholesalers now stood. We knew these places well. We'd ventured a little way inside one of the tunnels a few times, having found an entrance when camping out in summer. We saw strange beams of light and heard noises we had no language to describe. Another time, at dawn, we watched a convoy of trucks drive away from a long-abandoned building in the vicinity. There were signs and signals, too: wellies positioned on poles hammered into the turf; bottles of booze swinging from branches; arrows painted on stones. We watched cranes rise and fall like serpents in the distance, shifting endless quantities of indefinable matter for no clear reason. Once, we found a white door standing on a heap of slag—unsupported, like a sculpture, and obscured by mist. It was a portal, Dan said.

    We emerged from the trees on Geraint's street and walked to the end of the cul-de-sac, which backed onto more woodland, the last patch before the industrial swathe began. The driveway was empty. We knocked repeatedly, but the lights were off and there was no trace of movement. The old woman from the attached semi leaned out of her living-room window.

"Haven't seen him today, boys." Her bright pink hair tumbled about her weathered complexion. "His mam left first thing—saw her when I was fetching the milk, I did." We'd stolen milk from her doorstep a thousand times. "She was in a right flap—shouting at his dad on the phone about something."

We thanked her and lingered on the road for a while, discussing our next move. I suggested calling the police, but Dan thought it too soon for such drastic measures. Az reminded us of his firm belief that there was no such thing as an adult. We decided to revisit the factory instead and set off along the wooded path, beneath tight snarls of infected foliage. Crows cried from above, as if to tell us something. A red kite caused a commotion up ahead, then launched itself into the ether, the underside of its wings ablaze against the threatening sky. It soared like a comet back towards town.

***

The warehouse fizzed with activity—a normal day's work, nothing amiss. Employees marched in and out below the huge open shutters, heaving loads off a constant stream of vans and lorries. We watched from the fence, peering between the grass and brambles, waiting for any indication of either Geraint's or the caretaker's whereabouts. An hour passed before we saw the latter stroll from one of the portacabins to his shed, jangling a ridiculous set of keys from a tobacco-stained finger. He looked almost jolly.

"The fuckin' prick," said Az, clenching his fists. "He's got him in there, I know it."

"Nah, no way," said Dan. "Not with everyone around. Someone would have heard him."

"What if he's drugged him? Or gagged him? Wouldn't put it past the fucker."

A short while later, the caretaker stepped back onto the front porch and cast a wide gaze over his territory. The rain had slowed enough for him to lower his hood, revealing a head covered in erratic tufts, matted and feral. His expression, in contrast, was controlled, satisfied that all was in order and as it should be. Far behind, through the drizzle, I perceived the outline of a building I'd never seen before. This came as a shock—how could I have missed it? It was enormous. Was it new, or did the corrugated iron simply blend into the dark at night? Its sudden appearance was astonishing.

"Fuck it, let's kick the shit out of him." Az was raring to go. It was uncommon to see him so serious and fired up.

"No chance." Dan was more reasoned. "They've got security in the day—they'll catch us in no time and call the police, then we'll get charged for all the damage we've done. And you know what Ger's like. He probably just lost his phone, went to his dad's and couldn't tell us."

I wanted to agree, but it didn't seem plausible. The caretaker had him, I was positive. I forced a thought of murder back down my gullet like a gulp of bile.

"Let's go for a few joints and come back later—we can have a proper look around then."

We retreated into the trees to smoke, eat junk-food and wait for night to fall, so we could penetrate that increasingly bizarre realm and do our best to uncover the truth. I arched my back and squinted up through the leaves at the low, livery clouds; they looked about ready to burst and shower us with blood.

***

We sat in a triangle formation around a mess of burning crates, dense smoke swirling off the plastic ooze, engulfing nearby branches in pitch-black pollution. This wilderness had been a sanctuary to kids like us for years. We'd meet after school at the precinct, buy as much pot as we could afford from the teenage dealer behind Co-op, then disappear into this suburban jungle to make fires and chat shit with tribes of older tearaways, generous with their drugs and knowledge. They were sharp and resourceful. They could also be violent. I remember the time they drank spirits, fell out and fought amongst themselves. One cracked his jaw on the pavement by the church and needed surgery to piece it together again.

Dan handed me the dregs of our second five-skin spliff. I pulled on the loose roach, burning my lips, and felt a twinge in my throat—my tonsils were deteriorating. All of a sudden, my nerves flared. The plant life on all sides began to flick and shift, its breathing heavier than usual.

"What's that?" Dan jerked his head to the left, where the nettles and mulch on the forest floor crawled away to produce a clearing. Something was moving towards us, stepping purposefully over the scrub; twigs and branches crunched beneath its feet. My pulse thumping in my throat, I sprung up and staggered to where Dan and Az had risen, next to the fire. We watched the outline of a figure, broad and hunched, take shape in the thickening dusk and limp forward. Az crouched down and wrapped his fingers around a large rock. Me and Dan armed ourselves as well: a house brick and steel rod, respectively—the woods were littered with all manner of detritus.

"It's okay, lads, drop your weapons—I come in peace. Only me—Jammy." I breathed a long, too-obvious sigh of relief; Dan glanced sideways at me and clicked his tongue. "Havin' a smoke, is it, boys?"

Jammy was well known to us: a tortured soul whose fucked-up family had collapsed around him when he was young. He lived now between hostels and a tent he'd set up beside any of the various pillboxes in the area. His age was hard to discern, but he was over thirty, for sure. He was a warm, exuberant character; he loved to talk punk and metal music, and had no shame in smoking his way through your stash while doing so—not that anybody minded. If he'd been on the booze, however, he was best avoided. Alcohol roused his demons and he could become wildly unpredictable.

"Alright if I sit down? Been on my own for a week now—haven't seen nobody." The state of his Pantera hoodie seemed to confirm this: scuffed and torn, covered in mud and grass. There were weeds tangled in his famously unkempt beard. It was as if things were growing off him.

"Nah, not at all, boy—pull up a pew." Az was pleased to see him and immediately offered a cigarette. Jammy took it and sparked up, tilting his head back as he blew smoke out through his nose.

"Jesus, these woods are falling apart, innit?" He tapped ash on his combat trousers.

"Too right," Az agreed. "What do you know about the metals factory over there, boy?" He was wasting no time.

Jammy raised his eyebrows. "What you asking about that place for?"

We explained briefly about Geraint. He sat for a minute, digesting the information, looking at us carefully, probingly, in turn, and then spoke.

"Aye, well, doesn't surprise me, to be honest. There've been strange goings on down there for as long as I can remember. And that caretaker is a fuckin' psychopath—you wanna stay well clear of him."

His tone changed, calling to mind the precociousness of a child playing at grown-ups. "That man has got secrets few people will ever understand." He leaned closer to me, his stale breath infused with vodka. "If your lad's gone, he's fuckin' gone. You've got no business down there, now, you hear me—no fuckin' business at all." His face, I noticed, was covered in festering sores. "I'm tellin' you this for your own good, and I should fuckin' know." He stood up and lifted the front of his jumper, his pale torso weeping with septic wounds, larger than the ones on his cheeks and forehead. There were boils on his neck, too. "Don't say I didn't warn you." He took a plastic bottle from his pocket and slurped down the final sips of a clear concoction, before throwing the empty container onto the fire. "Steer fuckin' clear, you hear me?"

He kicked a clod of earth into the flames with a steel-capped boot and limped back into the trees, cursing under his breath and belching like an old sheep.

***

I came to on a cold stone floor, my limbs unresponsive. Sleep pulled at the back of my throbbing skull, dunking me in and out some obscure dream. The room steadied to reveal sacks of plaster, rolls of cable and adhesive tape, trowels and hammers, and packets of nuts and bolts. On a bench below the window were two drills and a glue gun. I could smell burning solder.

The last thing I remembered was running through the rain towards the warehouse, the caretaker chasing behind. I must have slipped in the sludge. I'd been determined to do my bit for Geraint and so volunteered to create a distraction, while Dan and Az looked around. I hurled rocks at the shed and set off to lead the guard on a lap of the site, but things had clearly gone wrong.

The door hinges creaked and a wet draft tumbled in. The caretaker stepped over me, took a length of wire from a hook on the far wall and yanked it taut. He was in his element here, surrounded by his tools—his means of altering the world and leaving a mark. He tied my wrists and feet, then lifted me with surprising ease, carrying me outside in his arms like a baby. His breath stank of eggs. He dropped me in a silver trailer attached to the back of a quadbike and started the engine. I vomited down my front.

We drove between vacant portacabins, passed the larger of the manufacturing buildings and arrived at a concrete glade. I was on my knees, my whole body shaking furiously with shock. Through the soupy gloom, I saw the beginning of a narrow dirt track, running up to that enormous barn I'd noticed for the first time earlier in the day. As we clanked towards it, the sheer scale of the apparition overwhelmed me. I was not conditioned to comprehend such magnitude. Its ramshackle roof was patched up with squares of different coloured metals, and the front shutters wore ancient coats of rust. Far off to the west, a motorbike blasted along the dual carriageway.

When we reached the side entrance—a conspicuously small wooden door—the caretaker disembarked and dragged me from the trailer by my collar. He dumped me next to the kerb, pressing my face into a foul-smelling pulp with his boot, before tapping the security code into a keypad fixed to the corrugated iron. He came back, flung me over his shoulder and marched inside.

I thumped onto the ground like a heap of meat, my cheekbone walloping into the paving slabs. I spat dust and sick from my mouth and turned my head to take in the view: the interior of this phantom structure was a single, limitless room—more like a stadium. There were rows of crunched-up barrels, and scatterings of what looked like bones. In the centre of the chamber was a vast body of water, black and iridescent, like oil. Above it hung a series of ropes and harnesses, all dangling from a ceiling I could not currently fathom. I tried to talk.

"Shut the fuck up." He kicked me hard in the ribs and strolled away, making for the lake. It occurred to me at that moment that I was probably going to die very soon. I thought of home and half expected to wake up; I urged myself to, refusing to believe this reality. Blinking tears from my eyes, I watched the caretaker veer off and approach a forklift truck twenty metres or so from the water. Suspended by a wire from the raised front bars was a figure, arms stretched above his head and trainers brushing the floor as he swung gently from his wrists. It was Geraint. I tried to say his name, but my voice had been replaced by a low rasping sound. I wanted only to run, but it was impossible. Instead, I writhed forwards, snail-like, in the direction of my friend. The closer I got, the more lifeless he appeared.

The caretaker mounted the machine and forced it into gear. He reversed a short distance, pulling Geraint with him, before advancing towards the pool. I did my best to increase my speed, but was stopped dead in my tracks by the sight of a hump breaching the surface of the glowing liquid. It was accompanied by a clacking sound, like a theme-park railroad. It curled the full length of its serpentine body briefly out of the water, scales of detritus emitting a rank stench and translucent gunge. It was as if the creature was made of material collected from a rubbish dump. I saw the lid of a tumble-dryer, clusters of aluminium cans and a faded plastic tiara all pressed into the flesh of this giant eel. I collapsed onto my stomach and shook my head vigorously. This wasn't happening—I couldn't watch.

The forklift engine cut out. My eyes were shut tight. They must have reached the lake and Geraint was either drowning or being chewed up and swallowed. The silence was excruciating. I waited for a sign of what was happening: nothing, then three swift pops and a deafening scream rang out. I looked up to see Geraint still tied to the bars, alive, dancing on tiptoes at the water's edge, his shoulders on the verge of dislocation. The caretaker stumbled, howling, from the driver's seat, clutching his face, purple blood squirting from what must have been a burst eyeball. Two more pops. He lurched backwards and raised an arm to protect himself from Jammy, who was firing on him from close range with a spring-powered air rifle.

    Dan and Az sprinted from a small gap beneath one of the rolling shutters and split up: Dan came to me, slicing through the ropes with one of Jammy's military knives, and Az went for Geraint. I got to my feet and the room started spinning. Amid the clashing images, I saw the enormous leviathan raise its head above the water, its eyes blazing. Az cut Geraint loose and, with Jammy's help, carried him halfway to the exit, where we were waiting. Once he'd handed him over to us, Jammy turned back. He raised his gun and began to shoot as he stamped away, shouting indecipherable words at the top of his voice.

    Geraint was barely conscious, his face pale as chalk and encrusted with sores. We took his arms around our necks and ran to the shutter, sliding underneath. It slammed immediately behind us. We hopped the nearest fence and fled into the marshes, crossing the boggy wasteland to the dual-carriageway, where we stuck out our thumbs. My tonsils were on fire.

    The night air was warm—sweat dripped from my armpit and trickled down my side. The town looked quiet in the distance, pylons humming softly in the fields. But the world was different now, I was sure. The skies cracked and there was a rumbling like thunder. I couldn't see the barn from where we were. I saw the woods, though, and a black shadow slithering towards them, clicking like a theme-park railroad.

THE BENCH BENEATH THE TREES

The green Vauxhall Corsa leaves town by way of the A48. It rolls past a drive-through McDonald's and a KFC, beneath a Victorian railway bridge, and comes to a halt at a red light on a large roundabout. Behind the car, to the east, an industrial estate stretches out like some alien organism, shifting its shape and colours to the beat of its own drum. Out west, along the coral horizon, which neither of us can see, are the steelworks, crunching and churning, spewing smoke over the channel from huge concrete tubes.

I press eject and remove the disc from the CD player. I replace The Refused with Joy Division and skip to the last song.

"I fuckin' love this," I say, lighting a cigarette and sinking back into the seat. "I fuckin' love it."

***

An hour or so earlier, I was squashed between three mates on a filthy mattress in a flat on the edge of town. The room was packed with boys from school, many of whom were in the process of making joints or cutting up lines of speed. Wisps of skunk fumes, like cirrus clouds, hung above and between us, clinging to the fibres of our clothes. Someone passed me an empty Fosters can, with a lit spliff leaning on the rim; my phone vibrated in my pocket.

Where are you? Fancy a smoke?

"Jesus Christ—what the fuck is that?" A commotion erupted on the other side of the room, by the door. Four of the boys, crowded around the computer, lurched back from the desk and spread out, circling something on the beige, ash-stained carpet. "It fucking bit me!" Joe was rubbing his arm.

Ben rose: "Urgh, it's massive—what the fuck is it?"

I popped the joint in my mouth and struggled to my feet, spirits swimming around me like silk. The boys were stooped low, peering through the dense fog at this evil thing. It looked like an enormous cricket, but its body was transparent, a plump abdominal bulge displaying an inner universe of throbbing blue matter. Its hind legs were thick and muscular, with sharp serrated edges, its forewings heavy as armour. Protruding from its face was a mosquito's proboscis. Somewhere amid the grotesque angles was a pair of pincers, fashioned from graphite.

"Jesus—it moves like a fuckin' fish." Laughing hysterically, Ben swung a rolled-up Kerrang magazine repeatedly onto the carpet, missing each time and scattering the boys left and right. Joe strode through the chaos, armed with a saucepan from the kitchen. He lifted it high above his head and heaved it down upon the creature, crushing it into a rich, colourful mix of slime and gristle.

"Have that, you fucker." He looked up, smiling. "God—my arm's fuckin' killing me." A purple lump appeared suddenly below his elbow and began to ooze.

With calm restored, the boys settled down, chatting shit and trawling the net, smoking and snorting, singing along to the choruses of old punk songs. I was feeling very stoned, caught somewhere between two worlds. I looked at my friends, their faces twisting around cruel jokes and cheap laughs. I saw the fag ends pressed into brown fluid at the bottom of pint glasses. There were yellow patches on the walls, expanding before my eyes. The smell was gross, like the steam off dead animals.

I took my phone from my pocket and began to type: *Yeah, I'm up the flat—come get me.* I paused for a moment and looked again at the smashed remains of the creature on the floor. *I'll be out in ten.*

**

The lights are green and we turn left, heading for the countryside. The car slides past a cluster of semi-detached houses and then rises over a stone bridge. The front passenger window is all the way down; in the half-light of dusk, with a cool wind against my face, I catch a glimpse of the verdant plant life bursting in spurts from the banks of the river, which itself is thrashing from side to side. It reminds me of a painting I once saw on a postcard in art class, its tones and textures so familiar. Tonight, though, the river's rage is real, palpable, and my fear is new.

We take another left and continue up a steep hill. The car pulls over to the side of the road, just beyond the village shop, and we step out onto the pavement. I scratch my arm and feel a flash of pain. I run my fingers over a lump, hot and tender, that's appeared from nowhere. There's liquid on my fingertips.

"What's that?" Sam asks.

"Nothing," I say. "A bite, I think."

We push through a set of kissing gates, covered in rust and cracked paint, and walk within the drooping foliage of an ancient yew tree. Sticks and leaves crunch like bones rotting underfoot. I look round and see the trunk is split apart like a wound, or the mouth of a death mask. Its crooked frame is hollow and deformed. Darkness spills from the crevice. Seconds later, I swear, its expression has changed.

We enter the playground and head for the bench at the far corner, which looks back over town. Sam slips a packet of skins, a pouch of tobacco and a small bag of skunk from his hoodie pocket and begins to roll a joint. The scene is almost totally still. I take in the view: the curving slide; the grin cut into the front of a large rocking horse; two shivering swings. Colours are tough to ascertain in this last gasp of light.

A gust of wind tilts the various play equipment askew and rips through the trees, which now lean over us on all sides. Streetlamps burn and shimmer in the distance.

"Do you know that's just one tree?" Sam nods towards the yew.

"Yeah, of course. Why?"

"The way it's broken like that makes it look like two or three, don't you think?" He's searching his jeans for a lighter.

"I suppose." I pass him mine. "I only ever thought it was one, though."

"Yeah, okay—but you know what I mean." He sparks up and takes a series of long drags, simultaneously exhaling through his nose. I marvel at this neat cycle.

"It does look fuckin' nuts, though, like it's swaying in slow motion."

"Yeah, like it's dancin' or something." He passes me the joint. "Don't you reckon? As if it moves to a different tune."

"To a different time," I suggest. "Like it's part of another world. The same as ours, but not—you know?"

Sam laughs: "Yeah, like another dimension. Fuckin' nuts."

The wind is blowing properly now and a groan creaks through the park. The roundabout rotates and the chains on the swings clink and then rattle. There's a rustling in the bushes behind us. A vole skitters from beneath the bench and veers away to our right, through to an adjacent field.

"Jesus Christ." Sam looks at me. His face is translucent—I can see his blood vessels.

There's a tickle in my throat and I begin to cough. It gets worse, unbearable, and I can't stop. I'm hawking and retching, desperate to relieve the itch, but trying seems only to compound the issue. I can't breathe.

My lungs are burning. I heave myself forward onto my knees and turn, pleading, to Sam, but he's writhing on the floor next to me, gasping and vomiting. Suddenly, everything stops. The wind settles and the grass curls. Thick coils of bramble unravel and creep forward. The trees arch, drawing breath. I close my eyes.

***

The ground around me is wild and alive, teeming with noise. I can see from every inch of my body's surface, as if my skin has sight, affording a stunning panorama. The landscape ripples like algae on a pond, ebbing and flowing, sprawling for as far as this rough skin can see. The atmosphere shifts from light to dark and back again, like I'm blinking, but I can't move a muscle.

I watch the ground distort, lines slashed into the earth: a sinister kind of symmetry. I drink in the sun's rays. There is pain and comfort. There is something blazing like knowledge, but I have no language to give it. The world around, the birds and the air, the creatures, heat and sooth like drugs. Stone is wrenched from the soil and stacked in irregular piles. I see smoke and fire, and pain radiates through my spine. My head is about to explode. An unbearable screeching sound, a scraping, will not abate. Something, or someone, is hacking at my guts. All turns white.

***

I am lying face-down on the wet turf. My limbs ache like hell. I cough a massive clot of phlegm into my mouth and spit it pathetically onto the grass. Sam is crouched with his arms folded on the bench, rubbing his streaming eyes into his sleeves.

"What the fuck was that?" he says, clearing his throat.

"God knows," I growl. "It was fucking wild, though."

I push myself onto my knees and crawl forward on all fours, baring my teeth. My skull is pounding. I stand up and stroke the blistered swelling on my arm. We take a few steps towards the gate and pause for breath. The breach in the centre of the yew's trunk has changed again, but into what, I'm not sure—a smile, perhaps. Together, we leave the playground and stumble back to the car.

THE DUNES

The darkness is deep and disorientating. Odd splashes of silver moonlight catch on the crests of waves barrelling from the south. The water is like ink. Twelve friends walk along the seafront in a broken line, their arms wrapped around one another's bodies. Some have paired off in conversation, laughing and sharing soaked cigarettes and cans of lager, while others have their heads bowed, as if ruminating on the way of things. At the front, driving the group forward through swirls of stinging spindrift, I tip my hood. I listen to the noise of the estuary and the gusts of wind. In the distance, to my right, the dunes are dormant, invisible behind what appears from here an impenetrable screen.

"Come on, it was funny as fuck—and brave, you gotta give it to him."

For the third time, Dan is dissecting the incident that took place a couple of miles back, on the cliff next to the castle. A crowd of fifty or sixty of us, from the local comprehensive school, had gathered in the cove to celebrate the end of term. We drank whatever we could get our hands on and ate cheap meat cooked over disposable barbeques. As evening dissolved into night and the encroaching sea pushed us back into the car park, others arrived and a mixture of punk and dance music blasted from someone's souped-up rear speakers.

"Stupid as fuck, if you ask me," Katie snaps over her scarf. "He was lucky to get away, like. That copper was a bit rough, though—I'll give you that."

The party had spread to the surrounding fields, near Witch Point, and into the castle courtyard, where two clans of smiling lads hurled lit fireworks at each other from opposing walls. A smaller tribe broke into the caretaker's greenhouse and filled it with bong smoke. Soon enough, the police were called and two riot vans came screaming into the countryside, to disperse the growing swarms. They were met with hostility: the bravado and insolence of teenagers writhing, ablaze, towards adulthood. Bob, Ceri's boyfriend, crossed the line with a barrage of insults and found himself spread-eagled on the grass, his right arm twisted to an impossible angle behind his back. Another lad, small and square, took a short run and dropped his shoulder into the copper's ribs, knocking him to his knees. Bob rose like a corpse from the ground and swung a wild kick into the fallen man's throat, before slipping through the mob into the woods beyond. Needless to say, we all fled the scene.

"A bit rough, be fucked, he was all over him." Dan takes a long drag of his cigarette and spits with expert control—grace, even—from the gap between his teeth. "He got what he deserved. Good on him, I say."

I approach the river, which runs from the town and splits this stretch of coast in half, and stop to let the others catch up. I feel a rock pressing through my shoe, into the sole of my foot, and reach down into a shallow pool of salty slime. Sensing some kind of significance, I wash away the grit and sand to reveal an indented swirl of pattern—a prehistoric mollusc or worm. The beach bends and ripples in the receding tide. A bulge of grey-blue cloud—nimbus, I believe—sags overhead, like a fresh placenta. I know this place well.

***

The child is dressed in a distinctive red anorak, which is zipped to his chin and chafes the lower part of his jaw. "I've got something," he calls, his face streaming with rain.

His father positions the pole carefully back in the tripod groove and steps towards his son. His shoulders are broad, his cropped hair iridescent in the mist. Looking through a box of old photographs years later, the child will be taken aback by the sheer size of his father's hands and feet, the length of his limbs. But here, with the estuary raging from the downpour in the night, he does not notice much specific about the man's appearance—he is simply there.

"Give us that." His father takes hold of the rod and presses the handle between his elbow and hip. "Snagged." His voice is low and without warmth—but soft, nevertheless. He releases plenty of slack and spins the reel. Suddenly, his wrists buckle and the rod convulses into an arc. He swears under his breath and, drawing his own father's pocketknife from his coat, cuts the wire. "Like it or not, you're doing this one my boy." He reaches for the tackle box and removes a large wrap of newspaper from a plastic bag. "You're bloody well doing this one."

The child looks across the river and rubs his teeth over his bottom lip. The air is thick with the sort of precipitation that hovers and twists like bedsheets blowing in the wind. His stomach contracts, sending a rush of liquid fizzing into his chest. On the banking opposite, he thinks he can see a body moving—a girl or small woman, perhaps. The man chooses a hook and two oblong lead weights, then turns back to his son, whose head is now bent askew; he's watching something, abstract and wild, thrash in the dense weather. The boy feels a hand on his sleeve. The man passes him the wrap of newspaper and sets about preparing the line.

***

"Have you heard of the Blue Lady, Ger?" Katie has dropped back from Dan and is walking between Sam and Geraint, her right arm stretched around the latter's waist.

"Fuck off now, Katie." Geraint clears his throat and swigs his lager, pushing her playfully from his side.

"I'm serious," she says, forcing herself back into the warmth of his embrace. "It's how Witch Point got its name. Haunts this whole coastline, she does."

"She's right," says Sam. "My Nain told me about this. Her and my Grancha used to leave this weird skull thing outside my door whenever I stayed at theirs, to keep the witch away. Nain joked it was her own father's head, but I'm sure it was a lamb or rabbit, or something. I fuckin' hope so, anyway."

"*Nain and Grancha*," Geraint mimics. "Call them Gran and Granddad, you freak." Sam strikes him hard on the shoulder.

"Yeah, anyway," Katie continues, "she was this Victorian woman who ran a clothing shop in town. One evening, during this terrible storm, she was calling for her son—four or five, he was—to come have his tea, but he wouldn't respond. She looked all over the house and ran out into the street, screamin' for help, but no one could hear her because of the weather. Eventually, in the middle of the night, with only a candle to see by, she found him suffocated beneath a pile of damp laundry in the corner of the cellar. He'd got all tangled up—probably playing hide and seek, or maybe just scared to death by the thunder."

"Fuckin' hell, Kate," Geraint says, shuffling in his pockets for his cigarettes and lighter.

"I know, it's horrible."

She explains how, consumed by grief, the woman fled into the wild, living in the woods and wandering the cliffs, crying for her boy to come back to her—and soon for any child.

"She was seen roasting rats and birds over bonfires, and singin' old songs and chants. She became known as a witch and the townspeople feared for their kids' lives. Then she disappeared entirely. Probably died where she was sleepin' one night and rotted into the soil. From then on, though, it was rumoured that if ever there was a storm, in the hours after, the Blue Lady would come back from the coast and scurry between houses, in search of a new child to love and cherish. She would drag them from their beds and lead them away into the dismal countryside, wanting to care for them but instead revealing some unimaginable horror."

Katie pauses for a sip of her drink. "The kids would be home by morning, looking the same as usual, but inside they were changed beyond recognition. Totally fucked up."

"Jesus," Geraint says, blowing smoke from his nose and flicking ash onto the beach.

"Good, ain't she?" Anna has caught up and pinches the cigarette from between Geraint's fingers.

"Yeah—Jesus," he repeats.

We turn and walk towards the sea, where the estuary is shallow enough to cross on foot. From there, we approach the dunes, an eight-hundred-acre sprawl of steep hills and low ditches, bracken and burial sites. Five miles north of this spot is my family home, where my mother and siblings will be sound asleep. At the far side of the dunes, nestled in the trees, is a ruined fourteenth-century manor house; it's overlooked by the Big Dipper, one of the largest sand mounds in Europe. Somewhere on the eastern flank, beside the river I intend to trace, is a water treatment centre, where employees, enlightened by their work, deal with the town's waste. As far as anyone can tell, they rarely leave the premises, other than to roam the scrub, dressed in fluorescent gear, collecting stories and messages from the ground.

Visiting once, a long time ago, my father explained that scenes from *Lawrence of Arabia* were shot here. He also pointed out where bombs were dropped during the Second World War; a nearby ordnance factory and series of tunnels built to store the ammunition were the targets, but a mysterious fog would invariably fall in time to obscure their location. Years later, my friends and I camped out in the concrete pillboxes erected to protect the tunnels. We found them hidden on the edge of a housing estate, overgrown with nettles and putrid with dog piss.

"Where to now?" Geraint puts his hand on my shoulder. "You're sure we can make it back this way, yeah?"

"We can definitely get back this way." Sam's jogging towards us. "You just follow the river to the sewage plant and then head diagonally across to the Big Dipper—the car park's right next to it and the road runs all the way into town from there."

Geraint pulls on the cigarette he's reclaimed from Anna and sips his beer. "Okay—let's get on with it, then."

The walk's a treacherous one and quiet soon descends. The terrain is uneven and difficult to navigate; as we leave the channel behind, we stride into an altogether more enveloping darkness. Looking around, I realise that all but six of our group have vanished into the night. Those of us left mount a long, meandering ridge, like the back of a sleeping reptile, and head for the river. The blustering offshore winds have fallen away and the peace is unsettling. I turn the fossil over in my pocket, fondling its grooves, and push through a corridor of thorn and bracken to lower ground.

Soon enough, in the distance, I can see the fenced perimeter of the sewage plant. An articulated lorry grumbles across the connecting viaduct, its full beams cast over the sliding gates. I check my watch for the time, but the hands haven't moved since departing the cove.

"Oh my God—that's fuckin' disgustin'!" Geraint shouts. "It's all up my leg! What the fuck is it? Urgh, it stinks!"

"Calm down, Ger," Katie soothes, taking his elbow and pulling him sideways along the track. "It's a dead sheep—a dead ewe. Wipe your foot in here." She shows him to a large tuft of grass.

"Urgh, I think I'm gonna be sick."

Anna, Sam and Dan are gawping at the corpse, which appears elongated, as if stretched out on some form of torture rack. One eye is hanging from a fleshy thread and its abdomen has been sliced open, spilling its steaming guts onto the sand. The smell is diabolical. We hover motionless for a few moments, before our trance is broken by a car horn bellowing from the direction of the town. Suddenly, as if injected with electricity, the sheep's legs kick and scramble; its lips part to release a long, wretched burp.

"Jesus," Anna breathes. "What the fuck was that?" We shrug and pull ourselves together, delving deeper into this alien realm.

We reach the plant and reset our course from north to northwest. We climb the hill on which my brother broke his leg in the snow, and I picture my father's wide frame emerging from behind a yew tree. This land is laden with phantoms. I pause and deviate for a second, to take a piss. A man in a hi-vis jacket ambles past, scanning the surface with a tool I've never seen before, his eyes fixed in a position that suggests a fugue state. He bends down and retrieves what looks like an old pocketknife from the sand; he drops it in a bag hanging from his belt and continues on his way. Far off to the west, the steelworks churn and grind to life, spluttering smoke and fire over the sea. The clouds have cleared and a sparse, shimmering light spreads tentatively across the dunes, illuminating our path. I roll the rock between my fingers and scrape its indentations with a chipped thumbnail.

***

The boy stoops onto his knees and places the bundle on the rocks in front of him. He wipes his palms in his jeans and looks across the estuary to where the figure had stood, but all seems calm. His father has cut the snagged line and is now attaching the weights.

"Be sure to pick a nice plump one," he says. "Plenty of girth—makes it easier to hook."

The child unfolds the paper to reveal a writhing mass of reddish brown ragworm, tasselled with hundreds of tiny legs and armed with sets of shocking black teeth, like graphite. He's sickened by their appearance.

"Quick now, lad. Take him by the top end, between your thumb and forefinger. Apply pressure and you'll have a good spot for the hook to enter, just below the head."

One of the worms is swollen, with a large bulge of lighter-coloured matter pulsing roughly three quarters along its length, fitting the spec perfectly. The boy avoids this one and chooses a smaller, less-obscene specimen from the assortment. The creature curls itself around his thumb, twisting hideously, almost turning itself inside out—as if aware of its destiny, he feels. He manages to suppress his revulsion and walks with his arm outstretched to his father, who is threading the wire through the eye of the shank.

"Take this carefully," the man says, holding the hook. The child's hand is trembling. "Take it carefully," he repeats, the volume of his voice rising. "Stop shaking." He reaches for the boy's empty hand and squeezes tightly, almost painfully: "Stop fuckin' shaking." The child takes a breath and tenses his muscles, working hard to steady his limbs. "Good. You'll go straight through the neck with it and then back in through the head." He sounds surprisingly gentle, reassuring all of a sudden. "You won't hurt it, I promise—they don't feel pain."

The boy does as he's told: pinching the upper section of the worm's body into a small protrusion, he presses the steel tip down until it punctures the taut skin, at which point the world around him dissipates. All he can perceive is liquid oozing over his fingers and a piercing squeal emitted, he is sure, from the creature's jaws. He feels a surge of blood rush into his skull and the estuary comes hurtling back. Through the mist, on the banking opposite, a woman is screaming, hair plastered to her face. Her blue dress is covered in soil and riverweed, her mouth gaping like a cave.

The child shuts his eyes, forcing tears to leak onto his soft cheeks. When he opens them again, the woman is gone. He turns to his father, who is now sobbing, his head buried in his enormous hands.

***

That night, the child dreams of currents ripping around jagged rocks, and of raptors crying from the crowns of trees. A kestrel soars overhead and alights upon a ruined castle wall. Eels slip through his bare hands and he slithers onto the dunes, his father's shadow flickering on the edge of this mutating space. The man's hoarse voice drowns beneath the babbling river. The boy locates the bones of dead crows buried in the clay and rambles into the woods alone, considering the lay of the land—there is no discernible way back from here. This dream is both exhilarating and terrifying; he longs to launch himself from the tallest peak, just to see what would happen, but he craves, as well, the warmth of home—to spread out and stretch on the soft, beige carpet. He wakes in his room and cannot move. A crude, animalistic breath rattles beside him. He cannot turn his head. His own breathing is too shallow, but for all the world, there's no reaching it. The woman moves swiftly on all fours from the door and climbs onto the mattress, straddling the boy's waist and soaking his pyjamas. She sits on his chest and smiles with rows of brown, broken teeth. Worms crawl from the knots in her black hair and drop onto his neck and face, squirming over the pillow. He gasps and lurches forward, into morning.

***

"I'm tellin' you, Geraint—she's real." Katie's rolling a joint while she walks. "I haven't seen her, but I know people who have."

"I've seen her," I say. "Or, at least, I've dreamt about her."

"Fuckin' hell," says Dan. "The first words you've said all night." He's smiling. "You okay?" I nod.

"See," says Katie. "She's fuckin' real."

We cross the final section of the dunes and begin a steady incline to the top of the Big Dipper from its rear. The sky has taken on a bluish hue. We pass the joint between us and, from the summit, look down on golden runnels of sand, frozen in motion, part of a different temporal flow. We can see the stream and, beyond, the empty car park where my father would change his shoes.

"Come on," says Katie, taking me by the hand. Together, the six of us run full pelt down the steep slope. The ground is impossible to navigate at speed and with such low light. Katie's grip slips and she's the first to fall away. I hear both Sam and Geraint call out as they lose their footing. Dan and Anna come careering on my left side and trip over one another's legs, tumbling off in a tangle of limbs. The wind is sharp on my skin and my heart thumps in my chest, like a drum. A chant rises from the forest. My limbs settle into perpetual motion and I continue onto the flat and into the trees.

    I come to a halt at the base of a ruin. The pounding rhythm has stopped. The walls before me are overrun with patches of dark-green moss and strips of ivy. Thick coils of bramble spill into a ditch that separates me from the crumbling structure. I lean forward, with my hands on my knees, and cough three times. When I rise, there's a woman standing in the doorway. Her eyes are closed and the bottom of her dress is sopping with mud and rainwater. Something moves in my pocket. The pressure of the rock against my leg, which has accompanied me for the duration of this night on the dunes, is no longer there. I reach in and feel the slithering movements of an enormous ragworm. I take it out and hold it in front of me. I hear rustling in the foliage and catch a flash of red. The woman opens her mouth, as if to scream, but there's no sound. I take a breath, kneel down and release the worm.

***

We're sitting in a circle on a flat rock overlooking the landscape we've just traversed. We've decided to stay and watch the sunrise. Dan and Katie have each rolled joints, which are now being smoked, and Anna has surprised us with half a bottle of vodka. The early-morning lustre reveals the cuts and contours, the angles and escalations, of the dunes. Things are clearer from here. Back south, the sea is beautiful, menacing. Something disturbs a flock of creamy-white seagulls from the banks of the river, and I can see a heron, I think. Far off west, smoke is expelled from monstrous grey tubes into the sky. I picture my mother, who will have risen from her bed and will soon be thinking about breakfast.

ASYLUM

The asylum lives and breathes in the wood. Of course, some of the trees have been cleared away and a narrow road with a roundabout now slices this particular edgeland in two, but still it's wild enough. The walls swell and throb, and warm moisture sweats from the clay and shale, seeping deep into the soil below. An unusually large community of slow-worms draws occasional environmentalists from afar, and the buzzards are huge—they crash talons-first into branches with almost reckless confidence—but this is generally a quiet zone. You can catch goshawks twisting erratic channels through boughs and foliage, if you're patient enough.

The hospital was built on the banks of the valley almost two centuries ago, to collect and contain the town's lunacy, and they'd have you believe there was much to be had. Gothic in style, arched and spired, it was dug into the earth with a cross-like primary structure at its core, around which a medley of buildings revolved (loops and cycles are very much the way here in South Wales): a church, an engineer's office, a farm, male and female blocks—a laundry ground attached to the latter—and observation dormitories, for the countless patients considered at risk of suicide. This landscape is one of patterns and repetition, of premonition.

One can stand now at the bay window on the top floor above the dining hall and watch the river wind and writhe through the valley, working its way to the castles and the coast. Brooks and streams cut further rilles into the land, but they are mostly obscured by trees. There's a ruined monastery to the west, dark and virile, and a smattering of stones survive in the graveyard, with hundreds unmarked. When snow falls, staff and visiting families make postcards of the grounds, and children toss orange balls into the cold air, their cries rooted and sane. A gowned figure at the far periphery wades bareback into the icy flow, into the grime and sediment of the town.

***

I dropped to my knees and scooped up a handful of topsoil. I tilted it back and forth, allowing the brown mixture to roll and ripple like river currents, before throwing it to the floor. Images danced and shimmered before me, of ravaged skin and pallid, dying eyes, puss-filled blisters. I have since learned that smallpox was here in 1962. It spread rapidly through the valleys, sinking into the sod and loam, absorbed by heaps of slag. I called for Sam to wait, clicked the advance lever on my camera and jogged on.

Two hours earlier, he'd parked outside my parents' house on the outskirts of town and tooted the horn of his dad's Ford. We were horror obsessed at the time and would often rent some obscure feature from the local Blockbuster store, pick up a pizza and drive in rings around the suburban edge, into the surrounding countryside. We were seeking new spots to pull up, smoke and watch on a small portable screen as the land rose to unleash its wrath and consume. The best part was then getting out to explore new and unfamiliar territory, blessed as we were with swathes upon swathes of nameless space to drift beyond the limits of our civilisation and *haunt*—to become spectres.

I was working on a photography assignment for school and so on this occasion we would forgo the film and return, instead, to where we watched *Red Shift* and *The Blair Witch Project* three weeks previous. We'd found an empty car park, perhaps more a muddy layby, near the woods that engulfed the old asylum, and we scared ourselves stupid; so much so, in fact, that we decided to leave the outside expedition for another night and, twitching with paranoia, headed home to bed. In the intervening weeks, the site grew and mutated in our minds, crying out to be conquered.

The project rationale was to focus on the uncanny. It was my first concerted effort to produce a themed series. I wanted to make the familiar strange, to take things—objects, natural features, buildings—that I saw every day and twist them to life, to tilt my world askew. The woods were perfect for this. I would see them regularly from the road—from the familial comfort of the car—but this known image, I decided, was a façade, behind which lay extraordinary mythological depth. And at the heart of these woods was the hospital where my grandfather had died—something I had long stopped thinking about. This was a journey both back and deep, an excavation of sorts.

"Look at this tree, man, it's split straight down the middle."

Sam was standing in front of an unidentifiable trunk, stripped of all but one half of its thick spine. The wood itself appeared young and healthy, its colouring lost in the darkness. I positioned my tripod and shot ten or so pictures from different angles. I paused for a moment and then approached the tree, running my finger along the smooth ridges of the cambium cell layer to the sapwood, where a thick, warm liquid spilled onto my skin. I snapped one more image; this time the flash threw its light onto the scene for what felt like minutes.

"Shit!" Sam shouted, and I saw it too: at the left-hand edge of the frame, an object or figure oscillating in the gap between two trees. Almost shapeless, it was black and floating, or was it hanging from above? The night returned and we stood suspended in film.

***

It's difficult to write now of my first visit to the hospital. It was so long ago. But I do recall bits and pieces of various car journeys there. Which, if any of these, was the first, I can't say. I remember with clarity, however, my initial steps into the ward. I can't have been older than nine. So this is an amalgamation, or montage, of sorts.

We reversed out of the drive and drove up the hill, past the cul-de-sac where my grandfather had lived not two months earlier. Through the window, I watched the houses—their flared vermillion brick and blooming cherry blossom—roll by in a familiar blur. We pulled onto a wide main road, passed the surgery and turned left onto the overpass that runs alongside the church—built in the 1830s—on one side and the brutalist recreation centre and council buildings on the other. We broke into a line of traffic and my dad, who had been silent up until then, began to talk about slowworms.

"They're lizards, in fact," he explained. "They shed their tails to escape predators. An incredible creature. They love the edges—of woodlands, fields and motorways. Formidable hunters, too. They'll devour huge quantities of slugs in single sittings. And they live for thirty years or so. Remarkable."

My three brothers were all in the car, the eldest eighteen years my senior. We continued past the local rugby club on the right, planted amid a dour-looking housing estate, and I was struck by the achromatic weather. Despite the spring flowers and pale sun petering between clouds, there was no punch to the arrangement before me. I wasn't sad about this; it made its own impression.

"Not long now," Dad said, and I—for some reason ignoring the fact we were still travelling at speed—reached for the handle and pulled, letting the door swing open. The car filled with clamour, wind and noise rushing down my throat. My brother scrambled across me and pulled it shut again, perhaps saving my life. I caught my father's eye in the rearview mirror—he was furious. I was terrified of him, and I loved him deeply at the same time. My brother patted me on the leg and apologised for shouting. Dad told him to shut up. The car turned into the woods and followed the narrow track over the roundabout, into an otherwise empty visitors' car park.

***

We stood stone still in the gloom, our shoes caked in mulch and clay. "What the fuck was that?" Sam whispered. He took two strides forward and peered into the murk, his whole body craning to the left. My eyes recovered from the shock of the flash and refocused on the vague figure swinging slowly from side to side. A twig snapped beneath my weight and a branch above the apparition released a long, high-pitched whine, like a cat.

"It's not a fuckin' body, is it?"

We moved forward together, taking small, tentative steps. I could smell smoke all of a sudden, thick and foreboding; it was filling my mouth and beginning to choke my airway. I coughed hard and, as if in response to the noise, the branch splintered and whatever was hanging from it dropped with a thump into the leaves below. Sam plucked up his courage and marched on. I stood where I was, fondling the body of my camera; the magnesium alloy was beginning to freeze—my fingers cold and aching. I heard rustling.

"Jesus Christ. Come see this."

Sam was holding a fistful of black and white Polaroids, as if a prime poker hand. He passed the pictures to me and continued rummaging. I flicked through sepia shots of faces like none I had ever seen before: torn images of cracked smiles and confused eyes, mouths agape and brows deeply furrowed. Some were staring directly and intensely down the lens, while others shifted their gaze uncomfortably away from the photographer. One man had the most appalling rash, wet and infected, raging across his forehead and onto the bridge of his broken nose. There was a girl, too, with shining hair and a laugh apparently filled with joy. A slug slid across her neck.

"They're someone's possessions, man, their life."

Hardly able to contain his excitement, Sam passed me three film canisters, a Parker pen and a yellow notebook with indecipherable markings scrawled wildly across the pages. Next came a woollen jumper—damp and foul—a rust-covered razorblade, a matching cigarette case and lighter, and a pair of tortoiseshell half-moon glasses. I coughed and cleared my throat. It was as if all this person had owned, or cared to own in their final days, had been stuffed heedlessly into a rubbish bag, but then hung in ceremonial fashion from this non-descript larch. Anywhere else and the objects would have appeared anachronistic, but here, outside of our usual reality, they belonged, as if part of the natural environment.

"Shit!"

A second thud echoed through the wood. We swung around to catch a final whip of sprung foliage, beneath which sat another bag.

"What the fuck?" Two more, three more, four more. "Fuckin' run!"

We scrabbled over a mesh of raised roots into a ditch and clambered out the other side. The woods around us were swimming in a deep-blue gleam and seemed to be leaning in on us. Unable to resist the urge, I glanced over my shoulder and saw, between constellations of black swaying orbs, a body, grey and crooked, lurching towards us. Flesh rose from my bones and sizzled. My vision failed me; I dropped to the ground.

***

He took hold of my elbow and walked firmly into the reception area. I had to break into a series of short sprints to keep up; I could feel his mood still seething.

I am remembering this, like so many other incidents from my childhood, for the first time here. I have recalled countless like it in recent weeks, with very little effort. In fact, 'recall' is the wrong word; I'm not *trying* to remember these things—they simply creep up and I'm suddenly submerged in a swamp of long-forgotten sensations. Sometimes I bask in these strange and familiar feelings, other times I splash and flounder for the shore. I was staring at my own reflection in a door knob last night, when the abrupt sound of him stamping up the stairs filled me with panic. The whole house would shake as I watched and waited for the handle to turn.

We walked down an endless corridor, school-gymnasium-like boards straining beneath us. A man in white emerged from a doorway and watched as we passed. He pushed a silver trolley behind me, its wheels clicking against the grooves in the solid oak. I remember kind-looking women arranging flowers and preparing medication as we veered into the ward. Dad had let go of my elbow by now and, instead, held my hand, stroking his thumb across my cold knuckles. He looked down at me, his expression warm and apologetic.

The room appeared an odd blend of cosy living space and industrial canteen: high ceilings, thick carpet; cheap plastic tables, deep polyester sofas; a large wooden television, around which seven or eight bodies were slumped, and a stack of dirty plates piled high on a second porter's trolley. A very old man, bent and limping, greeted my brother with a wild, pleading smile, bowing and ushering him further into the lounge. Another man, donning a full tuxedo, swore and then laughed hysterically, before kneeling down and pinching my cheek, a somehow tender threat therein. It felt to me like a circus—which, of course, is Latin for 'ring' or 'circular line'.

Hidden away at the far left-hand corner of the room, facing the bay window, was my grandfather, the back of his head instantly recognisable—it was identical to his son's. He was sat in a chair in exactly the same way as the last time I had seen him, with a racing newspaper splayed across his knees. One leg was stretched out straight, his foot resting on its heel, and his glasses, I could see, were tilting, as ever, on the end of his nose. Dad touched his shoulder.

When he turned, my heart broke into the first palpitations I had ever experienced. Despite all that promising familiarity, his physiognomy had been distorted almost beyond recognition. His bottom lip curled up towards his nose, his skin was grey and sagging, and he chewed methodically on his bare gums—the nurse would explain later that he'd lost his dentures during the night. Dad spoke loudly and in slow motion, and after a few minutes Granddad began to mumble in response. I heard my name in there somewhere, I think, and I'll never forget when he took hold of my hand. He squeezed hard and with love. I saw tears in my father's eyes.

***

A year or so after the night with the bags, I returned to those woods with four friends. We'd popped five Diazepams each—two I'd crumbled, absurdly, into the brown sauce lathered on a bacon sandwich—and eaten a barbeque at one of the boys' mum's houses nearby. She was clearly concerned. We took a tent into the trees and built a bonfire, around which we smoked joints and drank from flagons of cheap cider.

The flames grew and grew, and I began to lose myself. Someone was strumming three-chord punk songs on an acoustic guitar, and I flung my body here, there and everywhere. We swung ourselves around the blaze, undulating to an ancient beat beneath the broken sky. My friends wore animal skins on their faces: bears, wolves and boars. We laughed and howled in the moonlight.

At some point, I split from the group and walked alone into the dark, the earth below alive and boiling, scalding the soles of my bare feet. I put headphones in my ears, cranked up the volume and continued for hours, past derelict sheds and ruined walls, before collapsing against the base of an old oak.

I came to by the river, faint light and fog rising from the surface, a slowworm slithering between roots. I felt sick and lost, with an unparalleled ache for the comfort of home; I longed, and still do, to return. I thought of what my parents would have been doing at the time—of course, they were asleep, but I pictured them making toast with the radio on and heading outside to cut the grass. I stumbled to the riverbank and saw something glistening in the soil: an arrowhead, I was sure, but it was a bottle cap. I picked it up and threw it into the water. Two goldfinches were pirouetting in the shade of a crooked ash opposite, when out of the blue, I am convinced, a seismic wave rumbled through the valley. A hare darted diagonally up the slope to my left.

    I slipped my hands in my pockets and followed its path through bracken and thicket, to a stile beside a shattered monastery crawling with brambles. I climbed over into the grounds of the asylum, the river bending away to my right. Suddenly I stopped, paralysed, as if frozen by time. I could see a figure, straight and familiar, watching me from a distant window. I hadn't noticed the snow. My body turned to face the water.

ACKNOWLEDGEMENTS

Kestrels And Crows originally published by MIR Online, Lune Journal and Glove Magazine.

The Drive Home originally published by The Shadow Booth online and Lune Journal.

The Box Of Knowledge originally published in The Shadow Booth anthology.

An Orkney Saga originally published online by Elsewhere Journal and The Liminal Residency.

Nights At The Factory originally published by Black Static Magazine.

The Bench Beneath The Trees originally published by Porridge Magazine.

The Dunes originally published by Prole Magazine.

Asylum originally published by Black Static Magazine.

BIOGRAPHY

Tim Cooke is a teacher, freelance writer and creative writing PhD student. His work has been published by *The Guardian*, *Little White Lies*, *The Quietus*, *3:AM Magazine*, *New Welsh Review* and *Ernest Journal*.

His creative work has appeared in various literary journals and magazines, including *The Shadow Booth*, *Black Static*, *Elsewhere Journal*, *New Welsh Review*, *The Liminal Residency*, *Foxhole Magazine*, *Prole*, *Porridge Magazine*, *The Nightwatchman*, *The Lampeter Review*, *Storgy*, *Litro Magazine* and *MIR Online*.

He recently had a piece of creative nonfiction published in a Dunlin Press anthology on the theme of ports and is currently working on a collection of essays and a novella.

Tim won the 2018 New Voices in Fiction competition, run by Adventures in Fiction, and was a runner-up in UEA and the National Centre for Writing's New Forms Award, 2020.

He has had work included in an exhibition at the People's History Museum and his story *Asylum* featured in Ellen Datlow's best horror of 2019 list.

You can follow him on Twitter @cooketim2.

ADRIAN BALDWIN (COVER ARTIST)

Adrian is a Mancunian now living and working in Wales. Back in the 1990s, he wrote for various TV shows/personalities: Smith & Jones, Clive Anderson, Brian Conley, Paul McKenna, Hale & Pace, Rory Bremner (and a few others). Wooo, get him! Since then, he has written three screenplays—one of which received generous financial backing from the Film Agency for Wales. Then along came the global recession which kicked the UK Film industry in the nuts. What a bummer! Not to be outdone, he turned to novel writing—which had always been his real dream—and, in particular, a genre he feels is often overlooked; a genre he has always been a fan of: Dark Comedy (sometimes referred to as Horror's weird cousin). *Barnacle Brat* (a dark comedy for grown-ups), his first novel won Indie Novel of the Year 2016 award; his second novel *Stanley Mccloud Must Die!* (more dark comedy for grown-ups) published in 2016 and his third: *The Snowman And The Scarecrow* (another dark comedy for grown-ups) published in 2018. Adrian Baldwin has also written and published a number of dark comedy short stories. He designs book covers too—not just for his own books but for a growing number of publishers. For more information on the award-winning author, check out:

https://adrianbaldwin.info/

DEMAIN PUBLISHING

To keep up to-date on all news DEMAIN (including future submission calls and releases) you can follow us in a number of ways:

BLOG:
www.demainpublishingblog.weebly.com

TWITTER:
@DemainPubUk

FACEBOOK PAGE:
Demain Publishing

INSTAGRAM:
demainpublishing

Printed in Great Britain
by Amazon